THE KIDNAPPED SAINT

& Other Stories

by B. TRAVEN

Other books by B. TRAVEN
(Available in English)

THE DEATH SHIP

THE COTTON-PICKERS

THE TREASURE OF THE SIERRA MADRE

THE BRIDGE IN THE JUNGLE

THE CARETTA

GOVERNMENT

THE MARCH TO COABALAND

THE REBELLION OF THE HANGED

THE NIGHT VISITOR AND OTHER STORIES

P
3
.
K

PT 3919 .T7 A15 1975
Traven, B.
The kidnapped saint & other
   stories

Onondaga Community College

Syracuse, New York

THE KIDNAPPED SAINT
& Other Stories

by B. TRAVEN

Edited by Rosa Elena Lujan
and Mina C. and H. Arthur Klein

LAWRENCE HILL AND COMPANY

New York • *Westport*

ISBN: 88208-0490
Library of Congress Catalogue number: 74-9349

Lawrence Hill and Company, Publishers, Inc.

This book was produced for the publisher by
Ray Freiman & Company.

CONTENTS

Remembering Traven

by Rosa Elena Lujan

Traven and I lived together for about eight years in our three-story home in Mexico City. The third floor was strictly prohibited to everyone. It was my husband's studio, library, bedroom, and refuge. I was the only one allowed in "The Bridge" as he called it. Here Traven had the first editions of his books in more than thirty languages. There was also a large closet with many drawers filled with things he had collected in different places. In one drawer there were small rag dolls; in another Chamula hats; in a third there were brightly colored fabrics hand-woven by Indian women.

In the closet there were also arrowheads of obsidian which the Indians had given him. Traven went to the Indians of Chiapas as a brother, a friend, and a comrade, not as most outsiders did, to steal from or exploit them. Nor did he regard them as curios, but as human beings. The Indians recognized this. At night Traven slept on the hard ground with only his serape wrapped around him. In the morning he rose early and ate tortillas and chili with them. He was very good at languages and he learned the Indian dialects quickly. They accepted each other as brothers and exchanged gifts.

All over the room there were papers, papers, papers; anarchist papers, Wobbly papers, and scattered about were books like the Gotha Almanac, and a picture of Kaiser William II. All these things had significance and meaning for him, and I too soon came to appreciate their importance. For example, the innocent-looking rag doll takes us back to

Europe at the time of the Bavarian Revolution. Then he, using the name Ret Marut, together with Irene Mermet—both in disguise and in flight from the German police—made and then sold these rag dolls in the streets of Berlin to earn a few pennies and survive another day.

Traven and I had been close friends and were in love with one another since the early fifties, but we did not get married until 1957. I had been married before and had two daughters, Elena 12 and Malú 10 by my first marriage. Traven knew Elena and Malú from the time they were little girls. Before we were married they already loved him dearly and affectionately called him "The Skipper." After our marriage, when we all lived together in the same house, Traven told Elena and Malú "Our home is a ship and we must all cooperate to keep it running smoothly." At first he referred to my daughters as "your girls;" then they became "our girls," but very soon after that they were "my girls." He devoted much of his time and energy to them; he was patient and never patronizing. In some ways his love for them was strange; Traven had always been opposed to having children. His relationship to his own parents had not been good, and his early years were especially hard; he did not have fond memories of them. Also, he thought that the children of a famous person would encounter difficulties in life and he didn't want to burden a daughter or a son with his own legacy. Nevertheless, he was a kind and loving father to Elena and Malú.

Usually the "Skipper" came below ("Never say down," he explained because coming down meant shoving a corpse overboard into the sea) at seven p.m. He would have a drink —tequila, beer, or Scotch and water—and discuss politics, the news, or the girls' schoolwork. There was no censorship of topics and no forbidden subjects. The girls spoke freely about sex and religion, and he listened patiently always encouraging them. On other nights he gave them acting lessons, or taught them foreign languages, German and French. Elena and Malú loved to act with us. Traven made their education at home a game. He had them recite speeches from Shakespeare—like Portia's famous soliloquy—and in this way they became very good at speaking English and at the same time had fun. With silks and rags they made their own costumes and paraded around the house. Traven enjoyed it all. He had the marvellous ability to look at the world through the eyes of a child. And, of course, in his novels he was able to identify with people very different than himself—for example with the Indian woman who loses her son in *The Bridge in the Jungle*—and to understand and feel their sorrows and their joys.

We took Elena and Malú with us wherever we went, to showings of paintings and sculpture, to the ballet and the theatre, to conferences, and on short trips in Mexico to Mazatlan or Acapulco. On long trips abroad we preferred to go alone. When our daughters were away from home for long periods at school in the States or in Paris he wrote to them at least once a week.

In food he liked variety; once a week we would go to a French or to an Italian restaurant, the next week to an Arabian, German, or Jewish place, but most of all he liked Mexican and Chinese cooking. Traven discovered the most authentic restaurants, usually in the old sections of Mexico City he knew so well because he walked and rarely drove a car.

The so-called "mystery" surrounding his literary and private life rarely affected us because we had our own "private world." Of course, avoiding reporters from many parts of the world was quite a task. I was the one who had to face journalists, and I learned that they do not give up easily and do not accept a plain "no."

Traven disliked talking about himself. In this respect he was like many anarchists and radicals, especially those who lived at the beginning of the century and felt that they had no personal story to tell. They insisted that they only had a collective story, even though they were strong and sometimes stubborn individualists. I think that this way of feeling fits very well with someone like Traven—a man very much in love with communal life and communal thinking. He believed that individual stories are not important until they flow into the collective life. It seems to me that Traven liked to give contradictory and inconsistent information to reporters and editors; this was in accord with his feeling that his own personal life was unimportant. He said, "My work is important, I am not." He probably didn't realize what a headache he was giving scholars!

Sometimes, especially in his last years he did feel like talking about incidents from his past. I would listen fascinated because this was my only chance of hearing about the many wonderful adventures he had all over the world, from Chiapas to China. I rarely asked questions, though, because I knew that he hated them, and he would stop talking immediately. "Stop poking," he would say.

Some people think that I changed Traven. If I did it was certainly not intentional, because what I admired most about him was his ability to live the way he pleased. He always said that he would never let fame, glory, or money change him, and these things never did alter his personality or life style. Sometimes, Traven would say, "It's not good to be too happy. It's like having too much money. And if you have too much money it's because you have taken it from someone else."

Perhaps his habits changed most in that he lived a settled life with me. He had never been married before and although he gave different birth dates I knew that he was about thirty years older than I. So he was more than 60 when he married for the first time. We loved and respected each other exactly the way we were. When we got married we made a pact that each one would be completely free and independent. However, it was never necessary to impose this pact. Traven and I enjoyed working and traveling together. During our married life we were never separated for more than three or four hours.

He was the one who changed me; he gave Elena, Malú and me a new and different view of the world. He made us conscious that people were homeless and starving. Previously, I had had a sense of Christian charity, but not an understanding of social injustice and the need for basic social change. Traven gave us this important education.

After dinner the "Skipper" would go up to the Bridge again and work there until two or three o'clock in the morning, or until I came up "to interrupt him," as he would say. I would knock at the door, and not waiting for an answer—because he never answered—I would come in while he said, without lifting his eyes from the page, "Si, mi vida, I'm coming, I'll stop now."

We would have a nightcap together and decide whether

to go to our bedroom on the second floor of the house or remain on the Bridge and sleep among the books, and papers, and with the dogs. Yes, our two dogs were with him while he worked and he didn't have the heart to throw them out at night.

At breakfast—which was never before ten—Caroline, the parrot (all his parrots whether male or female were called Caroline), ate out of his plate. If she didn't like the food he was eating she would call him "Burro, burro."

After breakfast he watered the plants and took care of our small garden. One of his obsessions was to plant trees. He never owned land himself, but over the course of his life he planted hundreds of trees with his own hands throughout the Republic, no matter whose land it was or where it was.

He also fed the animals himself, including Lalo our monkey, who, before drinking the warm milk the Skipper offered him, searched his pockets for something interesting. Common things like eyeglasses and handkerchiefs were a bore and he threw them on the grass. Then my husband would patiently pick them up. But when Lalo discovered a box of chiclets he would shout and jump with delight into Traven's arms. Then he would fall on his back, holding himself only by the long, black tail circled around the Skipper's neck. Poor Lalo! When he fell in love with our next-door neighbor, a beautiful brunette, he became impossible and we had to find him a new home.

Traven also loved and respected dead animals. When our dear friend, the playwright Rudolfo Usigli was Mexico's Ambassador to Norway, he sent us three reindeer skins as a Christmas present. I thought that they looked beautiful on top of the rug in front of the fireplace. But when my husband saw where I had placed them he said, "No, no, I will not have anybody step on such noble, proud animals."

During our many years together I became accustomed to different things, and nothing upset or surprised me, including his different names and professions. When I first met him in the late thirties he was introduced as Mr. Torsvan, photographer, archeologist, and anthropologist. But in 1953 just before the shooting of the film *The Rebellion of the Hanged* I was introduced to the very same man. Only this time he was Hal Croves, representative of the author B. Traven. I was intrigued. He had written the script which I was to translate since the picture would be in an English as well as a Spanish version.

Later on he explained to me that he used the name Hal Croves for all matters related to films. I did not ask questions, and perhaps this was the reason he asked me to work with him. He told me, "We will shoot the picture exactly where it happened near Palenque in Chiapas. There are no more mahogany trees left there. It's a pity; almost all of them have been cut down. However, I found a few good locations." And he explained, "There are many stories by B. Traven which you can start to copy while I'm away; others I want you to translate into Spanish. Since Esperanza Lopez Mateos left us a year and a half ago all these things have remained pending, including some correspondence." He said all this in a sad tone of voice. I knew how much he had missed Esperanza, and how much he had cried when Gabriel Figueroa, the great camera-man and cousin of Esperanza's, told him of her death.

I had loved and admired the works of B. Traven for many years; so I immediately accepted the job he offered. I was thrilled. I had first read in English the Alfred Knopf editions of *The Death Ship* and *The Treasure of the Sierra Madre*. Later, I read in Spanish Esperanza's translations of *The Bridge in the Jungle, Rosa Blanca* and three of the so-called jungle novels. The first book I translated was *The Night Visitor and other Short Stories,* since there was to be a film in which three of these stories would be used. In 1959 a film which won many awards was made from *Macario,* one of the stories in *The Night Visitor*. Traven and I also worked together on many scripts; at this time of his life he dedicated most of his effort to films. Later, I myself translated the other three jungle novels, starting with *March to the Monteria,* then *Trozas,* and finally the last one of the six, *The General from the Jungle.*

On the third floor of our home there are many things— the rag dolls, the arrowheads, the Chamula hats, and especially the death mask of the Skipper—to remind me of a wonderful human being. He left us physically on March 26, 1969, but he remains alive in the hundreds of editions of his books all around the world.

PART I **Stories**

The Kidnapped Saint

Counting his savings on a certain day, the mine worker, Cecilio Ortiz, an Indian, realized that he had sufficient funds to buy himself a watch. To own a watch had been his great ambition ever since the storekeeper in the village had explained to him what miraculous things a watch could perform and what a watch was good for in every decent man's life, also, that a man without a watch was hardly a man at all.

The watch Cecilio bought was of nickel. It was very elegant, as everybody who saw it frankly admitted. Indeed, one could read from it twenty-four hours instead of only twelve, as with ordinary watches. And, as his fellow workers told him, this would be very useful if he ever meant to travel some place by train, since timetables would not say "7 p.m." but "19 hours" instead. In Mexico also the postal service, the courts, and other offices, as well as the theaters, use the twenty-four-hour time system, so it is very good and valuable to possess a pocket watch with twenty-four-hour numbering.

Cecilio was extremely proud of owning such a marvelous timepiece.

Of the Indians in his gang working side by side with him, and of all the others, he was the only one who brought his watch into the mine. As he frequently was asked the time, not only by his fellow workers but even now and then by the foremen of the various gangs, he found himself an important personage. Since it was his watch that had raised him to these heights, he treasured it as a top sergeant his medals.

One afternoon, he discovered with horror that his watch had disappeared. He did not know whether he might have lost it on his way to work or in the mine, because somehow nobody had asked him the time until the very minute when, leaning on his pick, he noted his loss. He didn't believe it stolen. No Indian in the village, let alone a miner, would have dared wear the watch, or show it to anybody, or sell it, or pawn it. Cecilio had had the watchmaker engrave his name, and had insisted upon very thick letters. The engraving had cost him two pesos and fifty centavos extra, but Cecilio had considered it a good investment. The watchmaker, who in his native country had been a blacksmith by profession, convinced Cecilio that for a watch there was no greater protection against thieves than the owner's name engraved on it, the deeper and thicker the better. The blacksmith had done his job so remarkably well that if anybody had tried to erase the name, the case itself would have vanished with it.

Not fully satisfied with this protection, however, Cecilio had taken his watch to church to be blessed by the señor cura, for which Cecilio had paid half a peso. He had hoped that with such double protection he would keep the watch to the last day of his life. But now the watch was gone.

For hours he searched all the nooks and corners he had worked during his shift. He could not think where he might have lost it.

Nothing else could be done until Sunday, when he could get help from the church and the saints. He knew by heart all the saints and their specialities. He would commend his trouble to the attention of San Antonio, as the one most intensely concerned with objects lost or stolen.

On Sunday he walked to town and entered the church. Having said a short and hurried prayer before the main altar, he went straight to that little dark niche where, upon a special altar, a wooden San Antonio stood in all serenity and solemnity.

For ten centavos he bought a candle, lit it, and set it up at the feet of the image. He knelt down, crossed himself several times, spread out his arms, and told the saint why he had come. Since, out of personal experience, he knew that a miner never gets anything without paying for it, he offered San Antonio four five-centavo candles, and a little tin hand, supposedly of silver, which would cost twenty-five centavos, and all this he meant to give to San Antonio as a reward if he would be gracious enough to recover Cecilio's watch by Sunday next, and not one day later, when he would return to the cathedral to learn what, in the meantime, the saint might have achieved.

His watch was not found, and Cecilio walked again to town on Sunday.

This time he went to see San Antonio straightaway without first, as was his duty, saying a short prayer before the altar of the Holy Virgin, for he was all excitement.

He crossed himself devotedly, stepped close to the altar, and when he did not see his watch where he had expected it, that is, lying on the altar right at the feet of the image, he lifted up the statue's coarse brown habit and searched among its many folds. He fumbled under the saint's clothes with very little respect, for his belief in San Antonio's power had received a severe blow.

Cecilio's candle and promises had proved of no avail. He knew that he would have to work harder on the saint to make him fulfill his proper obligation.

He bought another candle from one of the dozen stands inside the cathedral where one could buy practically everything necessary in the way of an offering to the various saints. There were all sorts of pictures, including photographs of the dignitaries and the señores curas of the town and nearby dioceses. There were leaflets, ribbons, tractates, books of religious and semireligious character, little arms, legs, ears, noses, hearts, eyes, donkeys, cows, horses, all of silver, or what looked like silver. Business, here inside the church, even during the regular service, was almost as noisy as a county fair. The church authorities had strictly forbidden trading during service, of course, yet who could allow five centavos to pass to a neighboring stand without some decent effort? Business would suffer, it might even go to pieces, if forced to abide by all the regulations it is loaded with.

Cecilio, too, understood his rights. He could well demand from San Antonio the return of his watch, if he complied with the proper formalities and promised the customary reward. Everyone worked for his food, even when too sick or too weak for heavy work, and Cecilio felt a certain resentment, and no mercy, toward the saint, who without working received such candles and prayers and trinkets of silver.

Again he set up his candle, lit it, and knelt down. He crossed himself devoutly three times. He had no prayer book, and could not have read one if he had. After all, knowledge of reading and writing only spoils the virtues of men born into this world to be good miners, who will never ask for more than they are given. So Cecilio prayed in a straightforward manner, just as the Lord moved his heart. As a faithful son of the church, he knew neither the words nor the meanings of blasphemy, which, had he known, he would never have used, no matter how far a saint might go in disappointing him.

Cecilio knew that the Lord knew best what was good for him, and could well console himself, alone or with the assistance of the clergy, for those prayers the Lord chose not to grant. But with saints it was different. They have lived on this earth and, therefore, ought to know how business is done in this world of cruel realities.

Cecilio knew perfectly well that he could not wait until after his death to have his watch handed back to him in paradise. He needed his watch here on earth. Paradise could take care of its time in its own way. The foreman in the mines of paradise would simply tell him when to ride in and when to knock off.

So, his arms spread out wide, Cecilio prayed, straight from the heart, as the Lord said, with little mind to the grammar or construction: "Oye, querido San Antonio, now listen my much beloved saint, and listen well, what I got to say to you here and now. I'm practically fed up with your goddam laziness. I am nearly through with you. Sunday last I told you confidentially that I had lost my watch, which cost me all my savings of silver pesos and for which I worked hard like hell, damn it, you ought to know better. Don't think that you can get away with it.

"No, santito mio, you can't get away with it just by telling me, as you perhaps mean to tell, that you don't know my watch, because my name is engraved in it, Cecilio Ortiz, and with big letters, too, and this name has cost me extra money besides.

"All this I've already told you already last Sunday. So see here, oh my beloved San Antonio, I can't come here every Sunday, as you might think and expect me to. I've got to walk the whole way, and under that blistering hell of a hot sun too, which is no pleasure, believe me. Of course, you standing here in a cool cathedral, you wouldn't understand this anyway. But I'm not lying about that heat outside.

"Besides, the candles cost money. I can't just pick up money on the street. No, most certainly not, the Lord knows it, just ask him if you don't believe me. I got to work and to slave for it. I haven't got such a good time in life as you have here. I don't just stand in a church, like you, doing nothing but count the candles the poor people offer you and watch how much money they put into the box. I tell you, this goddam laziness has to come to an end, at least where my watch is concerned. All of us have to work and so should you. The least you can do to win back my respect is go and find my watch and lay it down there at your feet, which I surely will kiss in reverence and in adoration for the good turn you've done me.

"There is something else, oh my beloved santito, which I must tell you and bring to your kind attention. One more week I'm willing to wait. But, listen, if by Sunday next you have not returned my watch, well, por Jesucristo, nuestro Señor y Salvador, I'll get you out of here and I'll put you into an ugly well for punishment. I will let you hang in the dirty water until you've discovered my watch, or told me in my dreams where I may find it. I hope you get what I mean and that I am in deep earnest. That's all and thank you ever so much for your kind attention. Oh, much beloved santito, pray for us!"

Cecilio crossed himself, turned his head toward the image of the Holy Virgin, said a prayer to Her, stood up, moved the candle nearer to the saint's image, gave it a last warning glance, and left the cathedral convinced that his ardent prayer had not been in vain.

But the watch was not found. Every morning, right after waking up, he looked under his hard pillow eagerly and full of hope. No watch was there. And none was under the bast-mat spread over the cot on which he slept.

"So you come through only for the rich, and never do anything for the poor," he murmured, "it seems that my compañero, Elodio Zevada, is right after all when he says that the church isn't good for anything but to make us dumber than we are already."

Cecilio had little talent as an inventor of new tortures. He had to rely on those he knew from bitter experience as a peon on the hacienda where he had been born and raised, until he had fled, and found a job in the mining district.

Saturday evening, after stealing an empty sugar sack from the back yard of the general store, he hurried to town. It was night when he entered the cathedral, and it was poorly lighted.

Crossing himself before the image of the Holy Virgin, who, so far, had done him no harm and whom he would not refuse veneration, he hastily said a short prayer, and, in a few added words, asked Her forgiveness for what he was going to do to one of Her companions.

With resolute steps he walked close up to San Antonio, whose altar, fortunately, was in the deepest dark, with only burned-out candle stubs in front, a tiny oil lamp at its feet, and not a single worshiper nearby. A score of women were kneeling before the main altar, their heads covered with black shawls.

In one quick move he grasped the image. Out of its arm he, very tenderly, took the child, which he put back on the altar; then, stuffing the saint into the sugar sack, he left with his prey by the nearest side door.

Nobody took notice of Cecilio hurrying through the semidark streets. In ten minutes, he had passed the last houses and was well on his way to the little mining village where he lived.

A short mile before reaching his village, he left the main road and trotted toward the bush.

The moon had risen, and the trail was fairly bright.

Ten minutes' fast walk brought him to a clearing in the dense bush. In the center was an old well, abandoned long ago. It had originally been dug by a Spaniard, who intended to start a plantation, of which still could be seen two walls of a building now entirely in ruins.

The whole place looked ghastly. Nobody, not even thirsty charcoal-burners in the bush, ever drank water from this well. It was covered with a greenish slime; the bottom was filled with moldering leaves and decaying wood. The shaft of the well, made of rock and brick, was inhabited by reptiles and other tropical fauna.

The loneliness, the ghastliness, and the reptiles had made this place the location for half a hundred gruesome tales of ghosts, crimes, and tragic endings of love affairs. The villagers avoided, as much as possible, the overgrown trail leading by the old well.

Cecilio did not go to the well lightheartedly, especially with a stolen saint upon his shoulders. Any moment he expected a phantom standing before him, barring his way, and doing something horrible to him.

But people madly in love, or extremely jealous, or very angry never do see or meet ghosts, at least not so long as their strong emotion lasts. And since Cecilio was very angry with his lazy saint, he most likely would not, on this occasion, have noted ghosts even had they celebrated a family gathering right on the rim of the well. He was desperate, Cecilio was, and blind to everything except how and when to get his watch back.

No saint has an easy life with an Indian. He who wishes to be chief of Indians must do what a chief should do, or out he goes. Consequently, if a saint wants to be worshiped by Indians, he must prove himself a true santito.

Cecilio was no savage. He did not start torturing his saint without giving him another chance to produce the watch. Cecilio's former feudal lord of the hacienda had been less considerate. His former hacendado had ordered his peons whipped or otherwise punished the moment a fault came to light, and the punished peons could explain their innocence on Sunday morning, at roll call for the faena, the extra work, mostly domestic, done all through Sunday forenoon for which work the peons were allowed no payment nor recognition whatsoever. And since punishment had been applied days ago, the peons scarcely thought it worth mentioning at Sunday roll call that they had been whipped without justification.

But Cecilio gave his prisoner every opportunity to make good. Pulling the image from the sugar sack, he put it on the rim, smoothed out its coarse habit, and stroked its tangled hair, making it look more decent. Third degrees usually begin with smearing honey on the defenseless victim's lips. The statue was about five feet high, but the head was that of a taller man in proportion.

Addressing his captive, Cecilio pleaded with him: "Now, santito, listen here, my beloved little santito, I respect you highly, you know that very well; in fact, I respect you far more than any other of the many santitos in the cathedral, except, of course, la Madre Santísima, you'll understand why.

"But something now has to be done about my watch. I'll give you one more chance, see, to come across with my watch. Be sure to be quick. I've done my part; it's now up to you to do yours. No more stalling, and no maybes either. Just take a look around, and see where we are at this time of night. You can see for yourself it is not very lovely. I may just as well tell you right now that at midnight it is a hundred times worse. Then hell is loose all around. You're the only saint who can find anything lost or stolen or mislaid. This the señor cura has told us many times, and he knows best because he is a learned man. I've promised you real cash besides. More I cannot do, because I'm just a plain hard-working mine laborer, which you can see here by my hands. I'm in the lowest wage class, too, and there is little chance for a raise as far as my foreman can see ahead, because he told me so.

"You know all this very well. I only remind you of these plain facts of life. It seems to me that you don't care for a poor mine worker, and less so, perhaps, if said poor mine worker happens to be an Indian, who is not of your smooth color and who cannot write letters and read the papers and who can make only a crooked cross when he gets his pay. I suspect very much that you're keeping hot company with the rich, working only for them because they can pay better. That's the plain reason I brought you here where we can talk plainly and discuss the matter quietly, if you know what I mean and you'd better know it.

"I can't pay as much as the rich and the goddam Americanos, who own everything here and all the mines besides, and to hell with them all. I do the best I can. But this is the end of it. I can't go any farther. I've spent my last centavo. Just take a peep down that ugly well. I tell you, santito mio, it's no pleasure at all to be hung down that well with only your head sticking out of that slimy and stinking water. Si, señor. There're snakes in this well. All kinds and sorts of snakes. Most of them are not safe to play with. There're other horrible things down there, too. If you don't recover my watch, down you go. Have I made myself clear, santito, or have I? I can't run every weekend to town just to see if you've got my watch hidden inside your frock or lying at your feet. I have other things to attend to, on the weekends in the village, with dancing and the women dressed up and looking after me to be taken into the bushes. No more candles for you from me, señor. By that I mean I'll give you right now just a very little idea of what you are sure to get if you still refuse finding my watch."

His speech was not delivered as fluently as it might read. Far from it. His mind worked ridiculously slowly, and more slowly still tumbled the words over his thick lips. But the image had no means to answer back and stop the Indian's blasphemous talk.

Cecilio's speech ended, and because he could think of nothing new, he started action. Out of his pocket he pulled a string, made a noose, and threw it over the poor saint's head. He fastened it firmly around the figure's neck, pushed the image over the rim, and lowered it halfway down the shaft. While the image was twirling round and round on its cord, Cecilio said: "San Antonio, answer, where is my watch?"

No sound caught his ears, only the singing, chirping, and fiddling of the insects in the bush.

Receiving no word, he lowered the saint farther down, until its naked feet touched the slimy water.

"Where is my watch, santito?" Cecilio asked, leaning over the rim and partly down, so as not to miss even the faintest whisper the saint might utter in his despair.

But San Antonio honored faithfully the high reputation of all good saints. He preferred to suffer at the hands of his torturer than to say anything.

Consequently, he was let down farther still. This time the whole statue disappeared in the water. Several times Cecilio would pull the image partly up and let it down again, covering, each time he did so, the whole figure with a slimy soup.

Having repeated his cruel game a half dozen times, Cecilio pulled the image fully up and stood it once more on the rim. "Santito," he pleaded, "you know now what this well is like near the bottom. I'm not so bad a guy as you might perhaps believe me. No one has ever shown the slightest pity on me, believe you me, santito mio. But I'll have mercy on you. I'll give you still another chance, even though you don't deserve it, because you are really very obstinate. I'll give you twelve hours more to think things over, and you'd better think them over carefully. Tomorrow, early in the morning, I'll be back here, because it is Sunday and no work in the mine. If by that time you've not recovered my watch or told me in my sleep, or by any other means, where I may look for it, then, muy querido santito mio, sorry as I surely will feel, I'll put you down again into this horrible well. I warn you, I'll put you down there, and all alone for a full week, because I must work and cannot come in the evening, when I'm dog-tired. After six days' suffering in the well, you surely will be ready to give up your laziness and stubbornness and do some real work for me, who worships you."

It used to be—that is to say, in certain remote regions of the republic—the custom to hang peons for twenty-four hours in an ugly well with the water reaching up to their necks as a punishment for alleged laziness, mutiny, disobedience, answering back, or whatever the hacendado or the finquero might have considered a crime against his sacred interests.

Cecilio himself had been hanged in such a well when once he had ventured to argue with the mayordomo about a certain order which, in his opinion, was impossible to comply with. So he thought that the saint had no cause to complain if a poor Indian worker did to him what the hacendados used to do to him and his fellow peons. No priests had ever interfered when Indian peons were cruelly treated by their masters, so why should he now show pity when treating in the same way a very intimate friend of the señores curas?

Having put the image back into the sugar sack, Cecilio hid the whole package deep in a thorny thicket. The habit of the statue was, of course, drenched, and Cecilio was aware that the poor saint would suffer terribly during the night, what with no protective walls of a church around him, and no lighted candles before him to warm him up.

"If you catch a cold, santito," he said in a low tone while hiding the figure, "it would only serve you right. I've given you plenty of opportunity to do your duty to me. Since you don't wish to speak up, well, there you stay until morning. Good night, buenas noches!"

On waking up in the morning, Cecilio looked under his pillow and searched the whole corner where his cot was set. He also fumbled through his pockets and examined carefully his wooden chest, where he kept his few belongings. No watch came before his eyes.

At an open kitchen on the plaza, he drank a cup of black coffee, ate a few tortillas and a plate of frijoles for breakfast, and hurried off to the bush.

He dragged the image out of the thicket and searched the damp frock inch by inch. No watch.

Once more he talked to the saint. But his speech was short, and his words were harsh and pitiless. He explained why he could not make a long speech and why he considered prayers wasted.

"You must know, santito, there is a very lively cockfight at ten in the backyard of the Ramirez cantina, and I've laid my bets already. In the afternoon I cannot come either. There is a dance, and I have a date with Borromea, who is my girl. You know Borromea quite well. One day she came to the cathedral and pinned a letter to your frock, begging of you that you should prevent me from breaking with her, which I had in mind to do on account of that old nag, her mother I mean, who is worse than a bruja and a witch. That is why I can give you only five minutes this time. If my watch is not here on the rim of that well inside of five minutes, down you go, and you'll hang there the whole week, until I come next Sunday to see what you have done in the mean-time. During the week I'm too tired from my work. I can't come before Sunday. That's all."

When Cecilio thought that five minutes had passed, he looked around and saw no watch anywhere.

"Now, I'll teach you a lesson, santito, how to treat a poor Indian mine worker, who is a decent Christian and who all his life has been faithful to you. But now I'm through with you. Down you go without further mercy."

Having lowered the statue until its feet were standing on the bottom, he tied the string to a branch of a shrub which had taken root in the masonry of the well.

It was on Saturday, early in the afternoon, when one of Cecilio's fellow workers, Leandro, came to him and said: "Listen, compañero Cecilio, how much do you pay me if I return your watch, which I have just found in the southern tunnel on cleaning up?"

"That's great of you, compañero Leandro, I will give you a half peso reward, and with my thanks thrown in."

"Sold," Leandro answered and handed Cecilio his watch. "Let me have the four bits tonight. There is your watch. No damage done to it. Just as good as new. Not even the crystal broken. On seeing something glitter among the heaps of ore, I took care to see what it might be. I knew right away that it was your watch, see, because your name is written in with big letters too. Besides, you told us that you had lost your watch and that everybody should look out for it in the mine."

Cecilio caressed his watch and covered it with kisses. Then, roaring with laughter, he said: "You do a lot better, compañero Leandro, and for less money than do the saints in the cathedral."

Next morning, Sunday, Cecilio went to free his captured saint. But the string was broken. The wind had moved the shrub about, and the constant rubbing of the cord against the hard masonry had worn it through. Cecilio could not pull up the image. Looking down for a while, he came to the conclusion that the saint had not merited the trouble it would take to climb down into the well to rescue him, since not the saint but an honest fellow worker had found the watch.

He leaned over the rim and shouted down the shaft: "Serves you right, santito, that the string has been cut, and that you'll now have to stay there for good. Perhaps the Madre Santísima wanted it that way. Good-bye, santito, adios. May the Lord have mercy upon you and help you out."

This prayer of Cecilio's, perhaps the most sincere and, since it was not meant for his own benefit, the most disinterested one he had ever uttered, reached heaven in no time.

Two charcoal-burners happened along the old trail by the well. They sat down on the rim to rest a while and light a cigarette. While smoking and talking, at times looking down the well, one of them suddenly broke out: "Why, for

God's sake, there's a guy drowned in the well, I can see his head and his thick black hair."

"You're right, partner," the other one observed, looking down the shaft also. "That's a man all right. Now, let me see, am I seeing things or am I? But that is not just an ordinary guy. It is a cura down there, I should say. I can figure that out by the tonsure on his head."

They hurried to the village with the great news that a priest had fallen into the old well and drowned.

Immediately all able-bodied people, carrying ladders and ropes, marched to the bush with the pious intention of rescuing the poor señor cura, who perhaps might still be saved if taken to a doctor.

It took some time to get the image up, because they did not want to hurt the poor cura by using hooks. Two men were let down, and, when they reached the image, they shouted up: "No doctor needed, he's stone stiff already, pull him up."

In the darkness of the well and in their overexcited state of mind, they did not realize what it was around which they fastened the rope. But as soon as the image reached the rim, everyone recognized the santito. All of the women crossed themselves, a few fainted, and a few became hysterical. One woman said to the crowd: "Can't you see what he wanted to do, our beloved santito San Antonio? He came in the middle of the night to bless the old well and had the bad luck to fall into it, praise be to the Madre Santísima."

In triumph and in a hastily formed procession, the image was brought back to town and set up in its former place, from which its disappearance a week ago had puzzled the town and had been the topic of conversation all over the county.

The señor padre in the cathedral was besieged with questions, and he finally had to give some answer. He was deadly serious when, at his sermon next Sunday, he referred to the strange event: "No human being will ever understand and solve the mysterious ways and doings of the Lord, glory be to God Almighty."

No better, no wiser explanation could he have given, because Cecilio no longer came to confess.

Submission

In a little town in the romantic state of Michoacan there lived a young lady of whom it could justly be said that a very kind nature had generously bestowed upon her all those gifts which greatly contribute to a woman's happiness.

Her father had been the owner of a prosperous saddleshop and through his ability and hard work had become very well-to-do. Luisa Bravo was the only child in the family. The inheritance from her parents, who had died a few years earlier and soon after each other, made her a rich girl, and there was every prospect that, upon the deaths of her grandmother and her aunt—both of whom had considerable means of their own—she would, in due time, become even richer.

Suitors fluttered around her like bees around a plate of honey. But none of them, no matter how urgently in need of money he was, or how eager to have such a beautiful and well-built woman to share his bed, held out long enough with her to get as far as an engagement.

This, certainly, was not the fault of the suitors. Where so much money, combined with such beauty, is at stake, everyone puts up with many inconveniences.

Luisa had all the faults a woman can possess. And two dozen more.

Her parents had lived in constant worry and fear that they might lose her, although she was as healthy and robust as a supply officer a hundred and fifty miles to the rear of the battle front. Ever since she was weaned, she had been spoiled and fussed over constantly.

Her every wish was granted immediately and her slightest desire fulfilled. Besides, since she was very beautiful, even while still a child, she was admired and flattered not only by her parents but by all who came in contact with her.

"Obedience" to her meant only the obedience she received from others, including her parents, her grandmother, and her aunt who, after her parents' death, lived with her in the parental home. She never obeyed anyone and no one ever tried to insist that she do so. (Such a case is very rare in Mexico where a child to the end of his life shows deep respect toward his parents and his elder relatives, and obedience is not even discussed because, quite simply, obedience is there. However, as Doña Luisa proved, there are exceptions in Mexico too.)

Her parents had first sent her to a Mexican school, and later to an American high school where she forced herself to obey as little as was absolutely essential. But she did not allow her basic character to be influenced by this in the least.

Here in the high school, it was only her vain pride and her abounding ambition to be superior to and ahead of all the other pupils, that made her condescend to obey. Yet once home on vacation, she made up for everything she had missed while gone, and she was more unmanageable than ever.

She had a violent temper which would frequently explode over the most ridiculous or trivial causes. The Indian servant girls and the boy apprentices in her father's shop would run away and hide from her for hours before venturing to come back again. Her parents usually smoothed over such situations by gifts and increased kindness toward the servants and other employees.

Nevertheless, Luisa also had some fine and noble qualities—among them that of being very generous and liberal. And a generous person, one who cannot bear to see anyone go hungry, and who is always free with a peso or with a pair of old shoes, or with a discarded though still presentable dress, is easily forgiven for occasional outbursts of bad temper.

Some days she was not only bearable, but unbelievably charming—so much so, that everybody smilingly forgot whatever she had done or said earlier.

Many young men, entranced by her beauty, and even more so by her money, thought that once married to her they surely would be man enough to insist upon being lord and master of the house. Yet as soon as they became better acquainted with her, they never dreamed again of trying to tame this temperamental woman. They realized that such an attempt could be made only at the risk of the tamer's very life.

Eventually, of course, like any other girl, she, too, grew older with the years. She had reached twenty-four, an age that doesn't look particularly good for possibilities of a marriage in which she would still have the decisive say. Generally, at about that age, a Mexican lady takes what she can get and endeavors to make the best of it.

Luisa's case, though, was different. She didn't care whether or not she was still among the eligibles. The conviction grew in her that it might by all means be better not to marry, since in this way there would be less trouble about obeying or pleasing anybody. Gradually she began to play with the idea—especially when contemplating her married friends and schoolmates—that for a woman with sufficient means, life might really be more agreeable and more satisfying if she weren't married.

And so it happened that in the same State of Michoacan there lived a man who went by the good and honest though simple name of Juvencio Cosío.

Don Juvencio owned a ranch not far from the town where Luisa lived. The distance was about two hours' ride on horseback. He was not exactly rich, but fairly well off, because he knew how to manage his ranch successfully and to good advantage.

He was about thirty-five, regularly built, of average appearance, neither good-looking nor ugly, but just about like any man who does not command attention and who hasn't broken world records in any field of sports.

Whether or not he had ever heard of Señorita Luisa Bravo will never be known. Whenever, as later on it happened now and then, the question was put to him directly, he simply replied: "Definitely no!"

Most probably this was true; yet undoubtedly it was also true that nobody had warned him against her.

One day, the idea occurred to him that it was about time to buy himself a new saddle since the old one had really become rather shabby. He mounted his horse and rode to town. Looking around, he came to Luisa's shop and saw the finest and best-made saddles in her talabartería.

Luisa had not sold the business her father had left her because she hadn't been able to get the price she thought the business was worth. As a result, she had decided to keep the shop and run it with the help of the old foreman who had worked with her father for more than thirty-five years, and with two married employees who also had been with him for many years. It turned out much easier than she had imagined. She busied herself in the shop and kept the books, while her aunt and grandmother tended the house. The business flourished, and since workmanship had remained equally good and customers had increased, the income from the business had become much higher than it ever had been in her father's time.

Luisa happened to be in the shop when Don Juvencio was looking at the saddles which were displayed, hung up at the entrance, spread out in the window, and along the outer walls of the building.

She came to the door and watched him for a minute while he, with the air of a connoisseur and a user, carefully examined the saddles for value, design, and durability. Suddenly he looked up and his gaze remained for a moment on Luisa's face. And Luisa, though later she was never able to explain to herself why, openly smiled at him. But she said nothing and did not invite him to enter the store to look at the saddles stocked inside. Neither did she speak to him in praise of her wares.

Her frank and open smile caught Don Juvencio unawares and he became somewhat shy. Still standing in front of the door, he said: "Buenos días, señorita, I want to buy myself a new saddle, perhaps even two."

"As many as you like, señor," replied Luisa. "Pase usted, señor, and take a look at the saddles which we have inside. Perhaps you may like one of those still better, since we don't display the good ones where they are spoiled by sun, air, and dust."

"Con su permiso," Don Juvencio said, and followed her inside.

He looked at all the saddles. But, strangely, he seemed to have lost the ability to examine them soberly and without prejudice. Though he tapped the saddletrees, scratched the leather, and made noises with the straps, his thoughts were only superficially on the saddles. He said little, and what he did say referred only to the merchandise.

All at once, he looked up quickly as if about to ask something. And though Luisa turned her eyes away immediately, he had caught enough of her glance to be well aware that, during the entire time, she had been examining him as searchingly as he had been studying the saddles.

Realizing that she had been taken by surprise while she had fixed her eyes on his face, it was her turn now to become shy. She blushed. But she controlled herself, smiled at him, and replied in a businesslike manner to his inquiry about the price of a saddle which he had just lifted from the stand and was examining in detail.

He asked the prices of a few others, but she felt that now he was only asking so as to have something to say.

He inquired about where the leather used for the saddles came from, how business was going, how many workers were employed, and other trifles.

Now *she* asked where he was from and how his affairs were doing. He introduced himself, told her about his ranch, about the number of heads of cattle, horses, and mules he owned, how much corn he had sold during the last year, how many pigs, and how prices had been.

For the moment nothing more was said about saddles.

After half an hour or so—neither of them had paid attention to time—he thought he'd better return to the subject so as not to make it too obvious why he had kept up the conversation.

"I think I'll take this one," he finally said, pointing to the most beautiful and most expensive of the saddles in the store. "Well, on second thought, I believe I'll think it over and have a look at some other stores in town. If you would hold this saddle for me until tomorrow, I'll come back and decide definitely whether or not to take it.   Bueno, hasta mañana, señorita."

"Hasta mañana, señor," said Luisa as he left the premises.

The fact that he did not immediately decide to buy was in no way surprising to her as a businesswoman. But with a woman's keen instinct, she knew that he had made his decision in respect to the saddle and had only postponed the actual purchase to have an excuse to come back again tomorrow.

Of course, he did not look at any saddles at any other place, but, as if in deep thought, strolled leisurely to the inn where he had tied his horse to a post, mounted, and slowly rode home.

When he arrived at his ranch he realized that he was hopelessly in love.

On the stroke of nine the following morning he was back in the shop.

When he found an elderly lady tending the store he felt as though he had been cheated. "Perdóneme, señora," he said after greeting the lady, "yesterday I looked at a saddle here. But the señorita in charge was going to show me some others, kept I don't know where."

"Oh yes, that was Luisa, my niece. Now see here, caballero, I don't know what saddles she might have referred to. She just went shopping. If you will wait, please, only ten minutes, she'll be back and I'm sure will be delighted to show you the saddles."

Juvencio did not have to wait the full ten minutes before Luisa returned.

Both smiled at each other like old acquaintances.

When Luisa immediately sent her aunt on some errand into the house, Juvencio understood that she, Luisa, was not disinclined to spend a short time alone with him.

As if it were only natural, he again commenced to examine all the saddles. However, conversation, apparently following an unspoken wish of both, soon turned from saddles to other topics.

Almost an hour passed in small talk before he realized he had to leave. He therefore decided to buy the saddle, took the money piece by piece from his vibora, that is, his coin belt, and laid it out on the counter.

Once she had taken the money, thus closing the deal, he prepared to ensure his return. "Señorita," he said, "there are a few other articles which I might need and if you don't mind, I'll return within a few days."

"This house is yours, caballero, return, please, whenever you wish. You will always be welcome, I'm sure."

"Do you really mean it, señorita? Or do you say it only as a polite business phrase?"

"No," Luisa laughed, "I really mean it. And to show you how sincere I am, won't you give us the pleasure of coming into the house and having lunch with us? You know, this is our lunch hour."

When Luisa and Juvencio entered the comedor, that is, the dining room, the aunt and the grandmother seemed to have already finished lunch, apparently unwilling to wait so long. And besides, they stuck to their regular hours for meals, being accustomed to Luisa's eating when she felt like it and not when others wished or even arranged to.

Yet out of courtesy the aunt and the grandmother remained at the table until the first dish had been passed. Then they offered a few friendly words to their guest, got up, and left the room.

Left to themselves, the two lingered nearly one and a half hours over luncheon.

Not the following day, but the morning after, Don Juvencio returned, this time to buy some saddle girths.

And from that day on, he appeared almost every other day to buy something, to exchange something else, to order something to be custom-made. That he had to sit down to lunch every time he visited the shop, soon became an established rule. Now and then it happened that he had to attend to some other business in town, which often delayed him longer than he had foreseen, and thus, of course, he stayed for dinner also.

On one occasion he had been unable to get into town until late in the afternoon. When he arrived at Luisa's it started to rain, so he was asked to remain for supper. But the rain soon became a heavy downpour. Visibility in the night was nearly zero, and the rain, instead of ceasing, grew more violent every moment. Why go to a hotel, the ladies said, and spend money unnecessarily, when he could stay at the house where there were sufficient vacant rooms? Even if the bed offered was perhaps not the finest, in no case would it be worse than the beds at the hotel. So it followed that he spent the long evening with Luisa and gratefully accepted their hospitality for the night.

Two weeks had passed when he invited Luisa and the elderly ladies to spend a Sunday at his ranch. Luisa and her aunt rode on horses which, early in the morning, he had sent into town together with two of his servants to accompany them. The grandmother, however, stayed behind to take care of the house.

From then on events took the course which they always take when a woman and a man believe that they might get along well in marriage, and thus put an end to the eternal coming and going which even at its best is really tiresome.

In accordance with the custom of the land, he politely asked for Luisa's hand in a formal call on the grandmother and aunt. Neither offered any objection to the marriage. Don Juvencio was a caballero of honorable family, fairly well-to-do, sober and hard-working, with all the virtues necessary to make a good husband.

Of course Juvencio had previously asked Luisa herself, and, because she had known since two weeks earlier what answer she would give in case he should ask, she replied, without hesitation and quite definitely, "Yes, naturally."

Her grandmother, however at times would say to the aunt: "Those two are still far from being married, and not until both lie snugly in the same bed shall I believe it. My advice is, don't bother about dresses or anything else yet. Besides, I'd consider it wise not to tell a single soul in town a word about the whole thing."

The aunt nodded in agreement for she was as skeptical as was the grandmother.

One morning, about a week later, Juvencio appeared at the store to chat for a while with Luisa. The conversation turned to saddles, and Juvencio said: "Well, Licha, all I can tell you is that you don't know a thing about saddles. In spite of the fact that you own a talabartería, I've forgotten more about saddles and leatherware than you'll ever know, believe you me."

This statement had been provoked by Luisa because of her insistence on being right concerning the quality and value of a certain type of leather, while Juvencio simply would not give in because it went against his better judgment. Being a rancher, he had had enough to do with saddles, harnesses, and leather in general to know by experience what kind of leather was of good quality, durable, and useful, or no good at all.

Luisa flew into a rage and yelled: "Ever since I was in diapers I grew up among saddles, girths, straps, and harnesses, and now you mean to tell me to my face that I don't know a thing about saddles and leather!"

"Yes, that I do, because it is my honest opinion," Juvencio said calmly.

"Don't you even dare to imagine for a second that you can order me about, even after we're married, which, by the way, I don't believe will ever happen. Nobody is going to order me about, not even you. And you might as well realize it right now. And get out of here as fast as you can, and never show your stupid face around here unless you want me to throw a couple of flower vases at you and give you a chance to think it over in a hospital. You'll learn who's boss around here and everywhere."

"All right by me," he said, leaving, while she furiously slammed the door after him, ran into the house, and shouted at her aunt: "Well, I got rid of that one also. Imagine, he thought he could talk and do as he liked. I don't need a man after all. Listen to me, I don't need a man. And he—imagine that peasant—he would be the last one I would marry."

Neither the aunt nor the grandmother commented. An occurrence like this one was no novelty to them. They did not even sigh. In fact, as far as they were concerned, it did not matter whether or not Luisa ever married. They knew perfectly well that, at any rate, Luisa would do only as she pleased regardless of what the two of them did or suggested.

Now it seemed that Juvencio was deeply and seriously in love with the temperamental girl. He did not withdraw as his predecessors had been in the habit of doing after an encounter of this type. One morning, four days later, he reappeared at the store. Luisa was unbelievably surprised when suddenly she found herself facing him. He gave the impression that he had entirely forgotten that she had thrown him out, and he seemed to be entering the store as usual, and out of habit.

Quite possibly Luisa, too, nursed in her heart deeper feelings for him than she had ever felt for any of her former suitors. While she was not exactly friendly, she did not reject him. And so it was, seemingly, only a gesture of courtesy that she invited him to lunch at the house.

For a few days, everything went well.

But then came an evening when she maintained that a cow could give milk even though she had not had a calf. She insisted she had learned this fact at the American high school. Calmly, he said: "Now see here, Licha, if you learned that nonsense at your American high school, then the teachers of that school are nothing but stupid old asses, and the knowledge and education you acquired there can't be very good."

"Do you mean to tell me that you are wiser than those teachers, you—you—peasant!"

"Wiser or not," he replied very quietly, "just because I am a peasant I know that a cow who has not had a calf cannot give milk whether you milk her in front or in the rear. Where there is no milk nobody can extract any."

"So you mean to tell me that I have not learned anything, that I'm a stupid fool, that I never passed an exam. Well, let me tell you right here and now, even though you are a peasant: Hens can lay eggs and don't need a cock for it."

"Right," he said, "quite right. Even cocks lay eggs when the hens haven't got the time for it, and mules even foal, and it is also true that many children are born without a father."

"Ho, so you want to contradict me and make fun of me! After all, I was studying while you were feeding pigs!"

"If we, and I mean people like me and other farmers, would not feed pigs, all your super-wise educators would starve to death."

She now flew into such a fury as he had never thought could possess any human being.

She screamed at the top of her voice: "Do you admit that I am right or do you?"

"You are right. But a cow that has not had a calf cannot be milked. And if there is such a cow it's a miracle. And miracles are the exception. In agriculture and cattle raising, however, you can rely neither on miracles nor on exceptions."

"So, on top of it you are insulting me?"

"I'm not insulting you. I'm merely telling you facts which out of my experience I know better than you."

The calmness with which he had pronounced these words incited her to even greater fury than a violent contradiction might have done.

There was a heavy stone water jug on the table. She

jumped to her feet, took the jug, and flung it at his head with all the force she could muster. Blood ran down his face in a heavy stream.

In a film, or in a novel worthy to be read by those who have a lot of time on their hands and very few ideas of their own, the young heroine would now have been deeply worried, and, sincerely regretting her rash deed, would have washed the wound with a silken handkerchief, would have taken the poor wounded head in her hands, covering it with kisses, and on the following morning both would have marched to the altar and then lived for the rest of their lives in happiness and contentment.

But since this was neither a film nor a novel, Luisa only laughed sarcastically, and, looking at her blood-covered suitor, said: "Well, I hope this'll cure you of your eternal stubbornness, insisting that you know everything better. And if you still have a mind to marry me, you may just as well learn this once and for all: I'm right, and I give the orders. If you agree to this, all right, and if not, then nothing will come of it, and, as far as I'm concerned, you and your superior knowledge and your ordering me around can all go to hell. Find yourself an idiot. With her, perhaps, you can do what you like. But not with me. Now you know me, or so I hope."

Without another word, she went to her room.

He went to see a doctor.

When Juvencio was seen two days later in town with a bandaged head, everyone knew that he and his bride-to-be evidently had come very close to marriage, but that now the whole thing was past and gone.

In spite of all gossip to the contrary, two months later Juvencio and Luisa were married. Evidently he had conceded that he would not insist on being right if she was of a different opinion, and he must also have agreed that she wear the pants in their married life. This was taken for a fact since, otherwise, the marriage would not have been possible.

The opinions of the young men of the town varied.

Some said that Don Juvencio must be an unusually brave man thus to place his head between the paws of a tiger. Others thought he had fallen into a kind of sexual dependency which had blinded him, and that he probably would wake up once his desire had cooled off during the wedding night. Others, again, believed that he had been guilty of thoughtless negligence toward her, and thus was obliged to repair the damage and marry her, even against his better judgment. And still others maintained that, at bottom, he must be very avaricious, and to such a degree that it made him overlook everything else. And then there were those who believed that perhaps he was slightly abnormal and fond of being under the yoke and the brutal power of a woman. No one, not even those suitors who had been after Luisa's fortune, envied Juvencio or were sorry they had not acted more intelligently while they had the chance. Everyone told himself and his acquaintances that he would hate to be in Juvencio's place.

Throughout the wedding festivities Juvencio's face was inscrutable. No one could tell whether he was satisfied with the world or not. But all the guests noticed that he always agreed to everything his young wife said. And if, during lengthy conversations the question came up, raised especially by the ladies present, as to how the two would arrange this or that in the house or in their future life, he stated that everything would be arranged according to Luisa's wishes. When, as the hours advanced, not only the men but also the ladies were somewhat the worse for drink, hints about the strong bride and the weak, compliant groom became more and more pointed, and it was even hinted that obviously a new era had arrived in Mexico, where at long last women had come into their rights. All these sly jokes which, at times, came very close to ridiculing Juvencio, left him as indifferent as the man in the moon.

One of his old friends, who had sipped more than he could manage, got up and shouted across the table: "Vencho, I think we better send you an ambulance tomorrow morning to pick up the bones."

Rude laughter was heard all around the table.

This was a very risky joke. In Mexico, bold statements such as these, whether made at a funeral, at a christening, or at a wedding, more often than not provoked drawn guns and shots (gatherings of the higher social circles are no exceptions). Hundreds of weddings have ended with three or four deaths—often the groom among them—and not infrequently, though only by stray bullets, the bride also.

But everything came off peacefully.

The wedding lasted well into the following day. It had been held at the home of the bride. When the festivities were considered ended, everybody was dead tired and sufficiently drunk so that nobody, including the newly married couple, thought of anything but of having a good, sound sleep.

It was quite natural, and nobody thought anything of it, nor did it seem against the established rules, that Luisa should go to her room to sleep, and that Juvencio went to bed in the room where he had already slept several times when it had been too late to return to his ranch. In fact, none of the guests had the slightest interest in what the two married people were doing, or where they were going to spend the next hours. Overtired, with full stomachs and brains drugged by drink, everyone had enough to do to care for himself, and had no spare thoughts to waste on his neighbors.

On the following morning, Juvencio, Luisa, the aunt, and the grandmother had breakfast together. Conversation lagged. The two women were in a sentimental mood because Luisa was now going to leave the house; and the newlyweds only exchanged indifferent bits of conversation about their horseback ride to the ranch and what would have to be done there most urgently to fix the new home.

Later on, the boys from the ranch arrived with the horses and the pack mules. Only the most necessary belongings for the first days of Luisa's stay were loaded on the mules. All the other things were to be transported later on by carretas.

Once at the ranch, Juvencio did not have much time to look after his pretty wife. A good deal of work had accumulated over the last days and had to be attended to first.

A ranch cannot remain idle for a day, or for a few days, like a factory.

With the aid of the old Indian housekeeper and the servants, Doña Luisa proceeded to arrange the place to her liking.

Night came, and when the time had arrived, Luisa lay down on the beautiful, soft, new, and very wide matrimonial bed. But who did not come to share that soft bed with her was Juvencio, her newly acquired spouse.

That this night passed like any other one confused her quite a bit. She had been told, and had heard, that there prevails a noticeable difference between being married and not being married, a difference which, in part, owing to circumstances rooted in psychology as well as physiology, can be agreeable—also useful to health and general well-being; or, however, can be disagreeable, embarrassing, difficult, unsatisfactory, undesirable, boring, repulsive, tiring, refreshing; or just turn out to be a matter of duty.

Luisa, however, had no opportunity to find out through personal experience in what manner and form the difference between being married and not being married operated. Because during the following night she remained alone again.

Now she became seriously alarmed.

Much as she wanted to, she could not fall asleep. Restlessly she rolled and tossed around in her cozy and so very, very wide bed.

It happened the following day in the afternoon.

Don Juvencio had been out in the fields since shortly after sunrise and had returned for lunch by noon. The meal was over, and now he rested in a rocking chair on the back porch of the large house. By his side, on a small table, was the newspaper through which he had been leafing without much interest.

On the same porch, some four yards away, Luisa rested in a hammock, a soft pillow under her head, reading a book.

Since she had come to the ranch she had not remained idle. She had taken her due part in all work that concerned her: the arranging, the necessary alterations, the general supervision and running of the household.

It was, therefore, nothing singular or out of the ordinary that now, after the noon meal, she should be resting comfortably in a hammock.

Since their arrival they had talked but little to each other. It seemed that both were testing the firmness of their ground so as to know in what channels their conversation was to run without spilling over. At any rate, this home did not echo with the perhaps honeyed but generally idiotic conversation which young married couples seem to be in the habit of exchanging during the first week or two.

The reason why no real conversation got going between the two seemed to rest exclusively with Juvencio. He evidently did not have the intention of provoking, during the first week, one of those devastating tempests if he could decently avoid it. But Luisa, with the fine sensitivity of the female mind, felt that something was brewing. That he had avoided her during several consecutive nights, as if she were nothing but a passing guest on a short visit, was too strange not to cause her to ponder deeply over it.

The day before, when breakfast had been brought into the dining room, he had asked: "Where's the coffee?"—"Ask Anita, I'm not your servant," she had replied rather coolly. So he had stepped into the kitchen, brought the coffee himself, and put it on the table without losing a word over the incident. Later on, she had made a terrific scene in the kitchen over the matter with Anita; but the servant had excused herself, saying that the master always wanted the coffee boiling hot and that she had been in the habit of bringing it to the table after he had eaten his eggs, and if the master now wanted it differently, he should have told her so, since it was impossible for her to guess his changing ideas. "Forget the whole thing, Anita, my fault," Luisa said, and with these words the incident was closed.

It was a hot, humid early afternoon. Though the entire length and width of the porch had a wide overlapping roof providing it with a cozy shade, it was beset, as was the grass-covered, ample patio, by a massive, immovable heat which made the air simmer, and which was bearable only if one rested perfectly still in a rocking chair, or swung gently in a hammock, thinking no more than was necessary to distinguish oneself from an animal.

Even the domestic animals which happened to be about were drowsing sleepily. They moved only when flies and mosquitoes bothered them more than they were used to.

On the porch, on a swing hanging from one of the roof beams, a parrot was dreaming lazily, waking up occasionally to shout or mumble some incoherent phrase, then returning happily to his apathy when nobody answered him.

On the uppermost step of the short flight of stairs which led up to the porch, a cat was fast asleep. Well fed, it lay almost on its back, its head hanging over the step. There it rested with that satisfied indifference shared only by those earthly creatures who don't have to worry about the safety of their lives or the regularity of their meals.

To a huge tree in the patio Juvencio's favorite saddle horse was tied. On the ground, a few steps to one side, lay the saddle, because Juvencio had decided to ride later in the afternoon to his trapiche, his primitive sugar-cane mill.

The horse, a splendid, noble animal, also was drowsing in the afternoon heat. Its head drooped inch by inch until its nose touched the few stalks which still remained on the ground. When its head finally descended low enough so that its nose touched the stalks, it lifted its head suddenly, opened its eyes wide, and realizing that nothing of special importance in the world had occurred in the meantime, closed them slowly, the head again beginning to droop as irresistibly as before.

From his rocking chair Don Juvencio could survey the whole patio. He lifted his arms, stretched himself slowly, yawned, and picked up the paper lying on the table by his side. He gazed at it for a few moments and laid the paper down again.

He now looked at the parrot which perched drowsily on its swing ten feet from him. While staring in this way at the bird, there came to his mind a story written by a certain Count Lucanor in the thirteenth century at the time when the Arabs occupied Spain and the Spaniards were deeply influenced by the Arabian way of living. Professor Don Raimundo Sanchez, Juvencio's teacher in advanced Castellano, at la escuela secundaria, had presented the story to explain with its help the curious morphological process certain verbs had undergone during the past seven hundred years. Thinking intensely of the story, Juvencio thought to himself: if the incidents in that particular story had the desired effect upon a situation similar to the one in which he found himself at present —and if the story told the truth at all, it should have the same result even today that it had seven hundred years ago.

And so, still keeping his mind on the story, he gazed hard at the parrot and shouted in a commanding voice: "Hey you, loro, hurry to the kitchen and fetch me a pot of hot coffee and a cup. I'm awfully thirsty, you hear?"

The parrot, awakened from its stupor by the words, scratched its neck with one of its claws, moved slightly to one side on its swing, and tried to resume its interrupted nap.

Don Juvencio, fixing his eyes more sternly on the parrot, yelled: "So, loro, living and eating in my house you refuse to obey and won't do what you're told to. I'll teach you a lesson right now."

He moved his hand back, drew his gun from the holster, took aim at the parrot, and fired. Feathers flew into the air, the parrot made a croaking sound, wavered, and tried to get a grip with its claws. But the claws opened, and it fell to the floor of the porch, beat its wings twice, and was dead.

Juvencio placed the gun on the table after twirling it a few times in his hand as if testing its balance.

He now looked at the cat which was so sound asleep that it didn't even purr.

"Gato," Juvencio called out, "hey, you, go and fetch me a pot of hot coffee from the kitchen. I'm thirsty."

Luisa had leisurely turned toward her husband when he addressed the parrot. What he said to the bird she interpreted as a joke and paid no further attention. But when she heard the shot, she twisted around in her hammock and raised her head slightly.

When she saw the parrot fall from its swing, she realized that Juvencio had shot it.

"Ay, no," she muttered in a low voice, "ridículo."

When Juvencio now called to the cat, Luisa, from her hammock, asked quietly: "Why don't you tell Anita to bring you the coffee?"

"If I want Anita to bring me the coffee I holler 'Anita,' and if I want the cat to bring me the coffee I order the cat to do it."

"As you like," Luisa replied, and snuggled back into her cozy Yucatán pallet.

"Hey, cat, haven't you heard what I told you to do?" Don Juvencio repeated loudly.

The cat continued to sleep with the absolute certainty that all cats, as long as there exist human beings, have an unquestionable right to receive their maintenance without in turn having to compensate for it with any useful work. It is true that, at times, they might graciously condescend to chase a mouse. However, they do not do so as a favor to human beings, but only and solely because even a cat feels entitled to fun that might not often occur in the regular performance of staying alive.

Don Juvencio, however, had other ideas as to the duties of a cat living on his ranch. When the cat did not stir to get the coffee from the kitchen, he said: "So, you don't obey my orders here? All right, I'll teach you a lesson."

He again raised his gun, took aim, and fired. The cat attempted to jump, but collapsed, rolled over once, and was dead.

"Belario!" Juvencio now shouted across the patio.

"Sí, patrón, vuelo," came the voice of the mozo from one of the corners of the patio. "Aquí estoy, a sus órdenes, patrón."

When the boy stood on the lowest step of the stairs, hat in hand, Don Juvencio ordered him: "Untie the horse and bring it here."

"Shall I saddle it?"

"No, Belario, I'll tell you when I want it saddled."

"Sí, patrón, como usted ordene."

The mozo led the horse close to the stairway and left.

For a while the horse stood in front of the porch. Don Juvencio looked at the animal as only a man who has to rely on good mounts can look at a horse, and who feels as closely linked to it as to an intimate and tried friend.

Several times the horse pawed the ground; then, perceiving that its services were not required, started, with mincing steps, back to the shade of the tree.

"Hola, caballo," Don Juvencio called after the horse which by now had gone about halfway across the patio, "trot quickly into the kitchen and bring me a pot of hot coffee and a cup. I'm thirsty."

At the sound of "caballo" the horse turned around because it knew its master's voice and was in the habit of heeding his call. But when it noticed that Juvencio did not rise and did not step into the patio, it knew its master meant neither to fondle nor to saddle it. It therefore continued in the direction of the shade tree.

"Now it seems to me you've gone completely crazy, enteramente loco," Luisa blurted out from her hammock in a tone that had a ring partly of astonishment, partly of growing fury.

"Crazy? I?" replied Juvencio. "I don't know why. This is my horse, and this horse lives on my ranch, and I order the horses on my ranch to do whatever suits me, just as you may order your servants to do whatever pleases you."

"Bueno, come tu quieras." Luisa's eyes returned to the book in her hands.

"Caballo!" Don Juvencio shouted again across the patio, "where's the coffee? Why the hell haven't you gone to get it as you've been told, eh?"

Hearing the familiar voice, the horse once more turned its head for a moment and when it saw, again, that the master did not move, it continued on in the direction of the tree.

Don Juvencio lifted the gun, placed his elbow on the table to steady his hand, took aim, and fired.

The horse trembled all over, stood for about a full minute perfectly still on the same spot, commenced to shake violently, and suddenly dropped as if struck by lightning.

"Thoroughly insane! Such a beautiful animal! Have you gone mad?" Luisa yelled.

She was filled with fury. It was absolutely certain that now the first big battle could be expected—the exact explosion about which Don Juvencio had received warnings from everyone. Had one of Juvencio's friends been present at this moment, he would have galloped into town as fast as he could to get an ambulance and reserve a bed at the hospital.

Luisa threw down the book she had been reading with such violence that some of its leaves went flying. She breathed heavily, commenced to simmer inside, and was just about to boil over when Juvencio slowly turned his rocking chair around in such a way that he was now facing her as she still sat in the hammock.

He did not put away his gun, but swung it up and down a few times, examined the cylinder, blew at the polished barrel, and rubbed it nonchalantly on his shirt sleeve.

And at the very instant Luisa was about to spring from the hammock to convert herself into a tigress, Don Juvencio said in a deadly calm voice, quietly and distinctly giving every word its full value:

"Get up you, woman, and fetch me a pot of hot coffee from the kitchen, and a cup. I'm thirsty. Hurry!"

During this speech his eyes had been lowered, but now he raised them and, gazing directly and coldly at her, raised his gun slowly, inch by inch, and finally aimed it straight at her body.

She caught his gesture just as she was about to spring from the hammock. However, she didn't spring, but slowly, almost automatically, slid from the hammock.

Now, pale as death, she opened her eyes wide and, after swallowing hard, said: "Ahorita, Juvencio, at once!"

Less than fifteen seconds later Luisa had placed the coffee in front of him on the table. He received it just as a man would who every day has his coffee placed before him by a waitress in a restaurant—as indifferent to it as to the price of the printer's ink of the newspaper he is reading.

Briefly he said: "Gracias!", slowly drank his coffee, and continued to read the paper where he had left off when he had felt thirst and had ordered the parrot to the kitchen.

"Belario," he now shouted across the patio, "saddle El Prieto. I'm going to ride down to the trapiche to see how the muchachos are doing."

When the saddled horse stood in front of the stairs, Juvencio got up, slid his gun back into the holster, crossed over to the horse and patted its neck affectionately.

Luisa did not return to the hammock, and even seemed to have forgotten what chairs were for. She stood as if petrified.

It looked as if she would need hours, perhaps days, to understand clearly what had happened. Not until many months later did she understand in full that in these few minutes her character had been completely changed—that she had lost all consciousness of her own self and acquired a feeling that no relationship existed any longer with the person she had been. For the moment, she stood there like someone expecting orders and ready to jump to execute those orders with lightning speed.

Before mounting his horse, Don Juvencio turned, looked at the leaves of the book strewn about the floor, and said in a light, amiable tone: "Licha, pick up the book. Day after tomorrow I'll take it to town and have it fixed again."

As he rode away, she bent down and, sliding about on her knees, picked up the leaves.

He hadn't used the pet name "Licha," instead of Luisa, since the evening she had bashed him on the head. So that when he now called her Licha and, in a tone which allowed her to feel plainly his unspoken "please," ordered her to pick up the leaves, she understood that Juvencio knew more about practical applied psychology than she had ever learned at high school. And so it happened that, under the impact of these few, intensely lived minutes, her character underwent another profound transformation. This second metamorphosis, jolting her into an unexpected awakening, suddenly gave her a definite feeling that she never before had felt: A fiery longing seized her for Juvencio's speedy return, because she wanted to be close to him.

During supper, neither of them talked.

Luisa went to bed. After a well-timed delay, Juvencio knocked on her door.

"Adelante!" Luisa said excitedly, almost shouting.

Juvencio entered.

He sat down on the edge of the soft, wide bed and stroked her hair.

"You know, Licha, you've got very pretty hair."

"You like it, Vencho?"

"Very much."

After a few minutes he asked: "Licha, who gives the orders around this house?"

"Why you, of course, Vencho," she replied earnestly and snuggled back into the pillows. "You, and only you!"

Three hours later she had acquired another experience, one entirely new to her. Namely, that even though in a household or a marriage it is not completely settled who is in command, still, in a bed in which a man and a woman lie side by side, the question of who gives the orders and who has to obey is never discussed, because it does not exist so long as the laws of nature are not set aside by some outside interference. Because in this situation satisfactory results will follow only if the man is in command and the woman subjects herself to his orders willingly and with anticipation. Furthermore, if in a marriage the woman is in command, it may be assumed with complete certainty that the man lacks the power of giving orders in bed in a voice so strong that the woman must obey and by so doing admit that hers is the submissive and receptive role.

In spite of the joyful and richly satisfying new experience gained by Doña Luisa during that night, she could not go to sleep as rapidly as one might have expected under the circumstances. She was plagued by a question.

Since women rarely can leave a matter alone which, in itself, is of no great importance to life in general, Luisa finally made up her mind to voice the question and rid herself forever of all doubts on a matter of great importance to her.

"Venchito," she cooed, "would you really have shot me

if I had not brought you the coffee? Would you have been able to do that to me who loves you so very, very much?"

Juvencio, considerably less bothered by such doubts, had already been three quarters asleep when the question brought him back to earth.

In an absolutely indifferent, cold, and utterly calm voice, he replied: "Now, don't you make a mistake, woman. I most surely would have shot you, and I would have shot you faster and easier than I shot my horse, believe me, I swear by God. For shooting you I would surely have been sentenced to death and shot, and that would have been the end of it. But as for my adored and beloved horse, I'll have to search far and wide before I find another like that wonderful, faithful, noble animal which I had to sacrifice for no other reason than to show you how deadly serious I actually was. Buenas noches, hasta mañana, good night!"

Everyone who is able to treasure and truly love a good horse, as a Mexican does, will understand without many words of explanation that this was the tenderest declaration of love that a man can possibly make to a woman.

The Cart Wheel *

Thirty-odd foreign petroleum companies operated in the Republic, among which the Condor Oil Company Inc. Ltd., S.A. was neither the most important nor the richest, but it certainly was the most ambitious.

Not only for the development of a human body, but for that of a capitalist enterprise, the possession of an excellent appetite is of vital importance, because it is the determining factor of the time that is used up and the velocity that is built up for the gobbling of money, that translates itself into power. Thus it is that the appetite decides the means that must be employed for a given enterprise so that this enterprise may come to be a controlling factor in national or international business affairs.

It was the youngest enterprise in the Republic and, perhaps owing to this reason, it had not only the most voracious appetite, but also a formidable digestion and a stomach which never regurgitating, was capable of holding whatever it swallowed intentionally, by error, by force, or by good luck.

This selection constitutes the first seven chapters of The White Rose, *a novel by B. Traven not yet published in the U. S.*

The ungodly fight among the petroleum companies in the Republic had a single goal, and this was to appropriate all the land that presented even the least possibility of producing petroleum some day, in the near future, or in fifty or a hundred years. The idea was to control all the petroleum sources, all the known ones and all the potential ones. Most of the companies put into play more power, more money, and more shrewdness in the acquisition of land than in the application of scientific resources for the exploitation to the limit of productive capacity of the land which they already possessed. Only by obtaining as much or more territory than that possessed or controlled by the really large companies, could Condor Oil hope that some day those companies that controlled the oil industry would seriously consider Condor as a real power in the oil market.

The general office of Condor Oil was in San Francisco, California, with various branches in Tulsa, Oklahoma, also in Pánuco, Tuxpan, Tampico, Ebano, Alamo, Las Choapas and Minatitlán, and it stood ready to establish new branches in the Isthmus, Campeche, Tabasco, Venezuela, and in the region of the Chaco.

A large section of the northeast coastal region, already proven to be rich in petroleum, was owned, leased, or almost completely controlled by Condor Oil. This vast territory was the largest and juiciest that Condor had been able to gulp down since it first operated in the Republic; and with the possession of this great loop of land, the Company had taken quite a leap toward the goal that it pursued, which goal was, to be considered as one of the dominant factors in the market.

Bordering and partly cutting right into the new Condor domain, were the lands of an old hacienda called Rosa Blanca.

Rosa Blanca occupied about twenty-five hundred acres of land which produced corn, beans, sesame plants, chili, sugar cane, oranges, lemons, avocados, papayas, bananas, mangoes, pineapple, tomatoes, and a fiber from which ropes, sacks, and hammocks were made, for domestic use as well as for export. Moreover, it bred horses, mules, donkeys, goats, pigs and something more esteemed at the place: healthy Indian boys and girls.

In spite of its expanse and its richness, the hacienda did not enrich its proprietor, Don Jacinto Yañez, even though it produced enough for a comfortable living. To a certain degree, this was due to limiting tropical conditions. But the relatively low productivity of the ranch also resulted in part from the fact that everything was planned and produced in much the same way that it had been done in the days when Don Jacinto's ancestors were still Totonaca chieftains in the Huasteca-land. The social and economic order of the hacienda was based on tradition and on the peculiar traits of the Indian race, and in that it was patriarchal.

Life on Rosa Blanca was easy. The human element was taken into account first and foremost in the hacienda's many affairs. Nobody ever got nervous or irritated or angry. Nobody drove, and nobody was driven. No sense of haste disturbed that angelic peace which made one think of a white rose in a flower garden never touched by man.

On rare occasions when some bitter word was exchanged, it was due only to the fact that man, from time to time, needs a change so as to better appreciate his peace.

All the ranch hands were Indians of the same tribe as Don Jacinto, that is, Totonacas. Nobody earned big wages. In fact, very little money passed through hands there, because the families that worked on the place lived on it, by it, and for it. Each family had its own house. The houses sure enough were of adobe bricks or of mud daubed onto a twig network, and they were roofed with palm-thatch, the same as most of the peasants' houses in the Republic. As the tropical climate allowed people to pass the whole day outdoors, year-round, the house was used solely for protection from rain or an infrequent cold wind. Moreover, to have built better houses would have meant more a nuisance than a comfort to these people.

Each family cultivated a patch of land whose dimensions were in proportion to the number of mouths it had to feed. The products of this patch were the undisputed property of the family assigned to it.

Nobody paid rent in any form to Don Jacinto for the houses or for the patches of assigned land. Moreover, each family was permitted to raise a certain number of animals, and to graze them on hacienda pastures. Any person or family suffering illness or infirmity was given medicine by Don Jacinto. His wife, as pure an Indian as he, had acquired some nursing skill at a hospital, so that she doctored some illnesses and acted as midwife in critical cases.

All the Rosa Blanca families descended from countless generations that had lived in this manner on this place. Rarely was a new family accepted, and then only by way of marriage. Most of the families were related to Don Jacinto in one way or another; not a few of them owed their presence in the world not only to the Lord but also to some of Don Jacinto's forefathers. Besides, Don Jacinto was the padrino, or godfather, and his wife, Doña Conchita, was the madrina, or godmother, of more than half the children born and living on the hacienda.

Being godparents of the children made Don Jacinto and his wife a kind of relatives of the children's parents, in a relationship regarded as more intimate and honored than that of mere brothers-in-law and sisters-in-law in that all the compatriots had deeply rooted confidence in their patrones.

Considering that Don Jacinto and Doña Conchita were compadres of the workers on the hacienda and that the most humble worker had the right to call paternal Don Jacinto his "compadre" and Doña Conchita his "comadre," it will be seen that the relationship between proprietor Don Jacinto and his "peon" workers was more intimate, say, than the relationship between foremen and work-partners, and much more intimate than the relationship that exists between employer and employee. Really, there were no social differences on the hacienda. Yet, while this extraordinary relationship wiped out the largest social difference, it did not wipe out certain traditional differences. Naturally, in this kind of relationship existing among Indians even before the discovery of America, there remained conditions not easily understood by those outside the Indian race.

A patron such as was Don Jacinto finds himself in legal possession of a hacienda that has belonged to his family for centuries, probably antedating Christopher Columbus for several hundreds of years. For good reasons, the Spanish con-

querors recognized the Indians' rights to the Hacienda Rosa
Blanca, and to hundreds of other native haciendas like it, in
that it was more convenient to have the native chieftains as
friends than as enemies. Being Indian not only by color but,
more important, by his heart, his soul, and his sense of justice,
Don Jacinto didn't consider himself the owner of Rosa Blanca
in the way that Mr. Crookbeak considers himself landlord-
owner of a ramshackle apartment house on Lehigh Avenue in
St. Lous, Mo. Oh, no. Don Jacinto considered himself only as
an individual to whom Providence had entrusted Rosa Blanca
for his lifetime.

No, he never really possessed the hacienda, he only had
the right to work it, and to work it not merely in his own interest, but for others, perhaps even more for those others who
formed the Rosa Blanca community. Yes, Rosa Blanca was
more than soil, buildings, and trees: it was the families who
lived on it and of it, and who, being born there, owned the
inalienable right to live upon that land, just as a man born
in the United States has, by virtue of the Constitution and
the accepted fact of his existence, the legal right to live in
that country.

≫ ≪

The same stroke of fate which converted Don Jacinto
into the temporal proprietor of Rosa Blanca, made him responsible for all the hacienda's inhabitants.

Yet he was one of them, scarcely distinguishable from
them; he dressed so little better than his compatriots that only
an Indian of the region was able to note the difference. He
wore the same sort of "huarache" sandals as did his compatriots. His meals, like theirs, consisted mostly of tortillas,
atole, beans, rice, green peppers; and orange-leaf or lemon-
leaf tea. Sometimes he would drink coffee, from Rosa Blanca's own coffee plants: coffee which was made in the Indian
manner with cones or piloncillos of crude brown sugar produced on the hacienda cane fields.

Yet, strange as it may seem, there remained differences
of a traditional character; Don Jacinto would not have seated

a single one of his peons at his table, not even his head foreman. The honor of sharing his ordinary meal was reserved for his immediate family and for honored guests.

No one in the Rosa Blanca community would have thought of consulting a judge in town, for Don Jacinto was the only authority in the world. A difference that appeared between families, be it the disputed ownership of a new-born calf, or even the case of a girl and a fellow unduly united, or perhaps the matter of a little inheritance, or whatever difficulty might pop up in their home life or ranch life, was submitted to Don Jacinto's judgment, and his word was the last word spoken on that case. Always, his decision was considered just and perfect.

No one of the community workers knew how to read or write but if it was necessary for them to write a letter or read something they received, Doña Conchita took care of it.

When the harvest was bad or when one of those regional hurricanes leveled the crops and houses, Don Jacinto was obliged to feed and house the unfortunate. In case of a death, Don Jacinto saw to it that the deceased was decently buried in the Rosa Blanca graveyard, where Doña Conchita would say the funeral prayers and then conduct the novenas in the home hut of the deceased. Don Jacinto took care of the widows, orphans, and the aged, often seeing to it that widows got a new husband, and that orphans got a new home that gave them not only proper care but also family love.

The land surrounding Rosa Blanca had been covered in part by forest or jungle brush, and in part by scattered ranches, hamlets, and Indian settlements. Condor Oil had acquired that vast territory when no one suspected that it might ever produce a drop of oil. It had been bought, or say, it had changed hands, not only by means of tiny amounts of money, but mostly by trickery, corruption of authorities, bribery of politicians, and by pestering interested parties as a swarm of gnats pester a peaceful animal.

The lawful owners were mostly humble Indians or "mestizos" who saw little of the cash that Condor paid for their land. In fact, Condor had spent very little real money for that rich terrain, in most cases as little as fifty cents an acre, of which the rightful Indian owners received, maybe, a dime an acre. When the native owners weren't clearly defined in the land records, and only about half of them were so defined, the money of Condor's so-called purchasing agents found its way into the pockets of all kinds of petty officials. The most frequent felony committed by Condor agents was the falsification of birth certificates, crediting assumed persons as legal inheritors of land which they allegedly "sold" to Condor.

Yet, this territory acquired so easily by dimes and deceit, had great value; a Condor's directors' meeting listed these tracts of land as their strongest asset, their indubitable property, in fact, their crown jewels.

Among these coveted jewels was a missing unit, Rosa Blanca.

Since the surrounding terrain had been tested and proven to be immensely rich in oil, there wasn't the slightest geologic or mineral chance that Rosa Blanca wasn't equally rich, if not even richer still.

Thus, Condor's president had two obsessions: one was to buy Rosa Blanca or to acquire it by any means, even the provocation of a war between the Republic and the United States; the other was the possibility (and it dogged the president and the directors' minds) that some stronger corporation, in better graces with the Republic's dictatorial regime, would grab Rosa Blanca from under Condor's claws, even while Condor brooded over that nest egg and considered itself the foremost option holder, who, having seen it first, also eats first.

During the months that the agents had acquired the lots and tracts of Condor territory, they hadn't overlooked Rosa Blanca, but had put off obtaining it. There were reasons for this. Unlike surrounding areas, Rosa Blanca was well cultivated and well occupied by many families, so that it was bound to cost too much in cash and in native dealing to get it. No agent or engineer was yet sure that the area contained oil; and whenever the question of Rosa Blanca came up, the agents agreed among themselves that if the surrounding area tested out and proved to be productive, they'd come around and buy Rosa Blanca, even if it cost a bit more. After all, who was

Don Jacinto but an ignorant Indian, a native hick with his bare feet sticking out of homemade sandals, and the agents were sure he'd be damned happy to see a few hundred dollars heaped up in front of him in cold cash, in shiny gold and silver.

But now the first five wells around the hacienda had come in, like geysers. And the agents hurried to offer Don Jacinto a yearly lease of two dollars an acre. Yes, sir, and renewable each year. Don Jacinto didn't say yes and he didn't say no, and in two hours he had forgotten their offer.

A few weeks later they offered him two dollars an acre in yearly rent, and they'd give him a twenty-year lease if he'd sign on the dotted line. Again, he forgot it. Three months went by and a new offer was made; a twenty-year contract-lease plus one percent of gross oil production on the place. Don Jacinto said nothing to that offer. Two months later they repeated the offer, but ante'd up to eight percent on the share Don Jacinto was to get.

A Señor Pallares, who acted as head agent for Condor, had come in person with this final offer.

"Sí, señor, the proposition is magnificent, I admit," said Don Jacinto earnestly, "but I'm sorry that I can't accept it, as you advise. You see, señor, it's not for me to lease this hacienda, because I have no right to lease it. My father never dreamed of leasing our land, neither did my grandfather nor his grandfather. I'm bound to keep Rosa Blanca and guard it for those who'll be here after I'm gone, and for others who'll follow those."

"Sure thing," said Señor Pallares, quite bored. For he had understood almost nothing of Don Jacinto's sincere explanation. He was a businessman to whom land was money, and nothing more. He himself neither owned land, nor worked it, nor did his family. Besides dealing in land, he played politics and hoped to be elected a deputy in the national congress, some day, if only he could make enough money out of land deals to pay his election expenses.

Now, he wrote to Condor Oil that Don Jacinto seemed to be crazy.

"That's wonderful!" exclaimed the Condor vice-president, on reading the report. "If that lousy Indian is crazy, we ought to have him put into the nut house, and leave him there until he rots, for the benefit of mankind."

⤳ ⤲

Soon another agent, a certain Licenciado (D.C.L.) Pérez appeared at Rosa Blanca on behalf of Condor Oil. He brought a canvas bag that was bulging with money. It wasn't all the money that Condor was ready to pay Don Jacinto, but it certainly was enough to make most men change their minds on almost any matter, including their religious belief.

This lawyer Pérez no longer offered a Condor lease, for the Company directors now proposed to buy the hacienda outright; and so they offered more money. Plenty more, so that Don Jacinto couldn't possibly turn it down.

"But look here, mister lawyer, how could I sell Rosa Blanca?" Don Jacinto asked in his usual quiet manner. Time was no object to him. He took his time when speaking to his wife, to his children, to his foreman, to his compadres, to cattle traders, to merchants, and nobody and nothing could make him hurry. "Really, Señor Licenciado, as I said before, I'm sorry to disappoint you, but you see it's impossible for me to sell Rosa Blanca, because it really doesn't belong to me."

Señor Pérez straightened up in his chair, stuck a finger into his ear and screwed it around like a clown and blinked stupidly into Don Jacinto's face. Then he gasped, "Must I believe my ears? Or is something wrong with my hearing? You mean to say that you're not the real owner of Rosa Blanca?"

Now, lawyer Pérez was Condor's chief agent in the region, and he was well paid to represent the Company before the legal authorities of the Republic. Could it be that he, astute and able lawyer that he was, had overlooked a basic premise such as this, that this Indian wasn't Rosa Blanca's legal owner? Impossible! If so, it would change the whole business overnight. Actually, half the properties acquired by foreign oil and mining exploiters had been bought at ridiculously low prices, due to the fact that few owners could prove ownership by means of legal documents. Hundreds of holdings in the Republic, though occupied by the same family for successive generations, never had been recorded anywhere, except at the tax office, where they didn't question as to who owned this or that as long as the stipulated taxes were paid punctually. Thus, a property as important as Rosa Blanca could be declared abandoned, or claimed as property of the nation, and the governor or some political boss could sell the property at a fake auction for ten thousand dollars, and realize maybe a hundred thousand on it.

Sweat poured from Señor Pérez's face, and he excitedly mopped and fanned it with a huge handkerchief. Still gasping, he stammered, "What I can't . . . that is, I mean . . . yes, I myself have gone through the land deeds and records of this property, Don Jacinto. And I'm able to say that I found not the slightest error in documents, some of which were dated in the sixteenth century. We did have to get expert translators to render the old Castilian documents into modern Spanish. And not one error, not one omission was to be found anywhere! Yes, you are the legal owner, Don Jacinto, beyond the shadow of doubt. Frankly speaking, I'll tell you that I wished you weren't the legal owner!" and the lawyer gave him a big grin.

"Clearly, I'm the rightful owner. Who said I wasn't?"

"But you just finished saying, a minute ago, that Rosa Blanca wasn't yours!"

"Sí. I said that, meaning it in a different way. The place is mine. But not mine to the degree that I can do with it as I please."

"But why in God's name can't you, Don Jacinto?"

"I'll try to explain it clearly, Señor Licenciado. Of course I cultivate the land, I grow on it what's good for all of us, but still I'm not the sole owner, here. My father owned the land as I own it now, and as my eldest son will own it someday, when I've departed. See, it really didn't belong to my father, for he had to hand it on to me, and I will have to hand it on to my son, when I'm called away from here."

"Don Jacinto, get off the stupidities. As for your children, here's the money to make them happy—or, if you prefer, you could will it to them. You've got fine daughters and sons—you want them to rot here like common Indians?

They're young! They want to enjoy life. Why make them field-hands and herdsmen, when they could be cultured citizens? Doctors. Or lawyers, like me. Engineers. Architects. Merchants. Capable of living decently in a civilized city, eh? Or, if they don't like to study, they'd still be able to just live, to buy all those fine things that money buys, things made just for people with money!"

"Could be," said Don Jacinto curtly. "Yes, it could be, Señor Licenciado. Except that they'd be landless. They're human, and have to eat. And how could they eat if they didn't grow maize corn, frijoles, and fruit?"

"Don't talk nonsense, Don Jacinto. Your children could buy all the corn and frijoles they need. They'd be able to buy or do anything, with these thousands of pesos we're going to give you for the land, eh?"

Don Jacinto didn't answer. He couldn't think as rapidly as these lawyers, his thoughts couldn't catch up with such a rush of arguments. Realizing this, Pérez decided to convince the balky Indian by another tactic, such as he'd used successfully on handling other stubborn country people.

"Look, Don Jacinto, some day you'll be old and infirm, and ready to take it easy, eh?"

"I, old and infirm? Never. I don't age. The day when I get what you call 'old,' I'll die without a whimper. And something more ought to be considered, Señor Licenciado Pérez."

"Well, speak, Don Jacinto. I came to hear you out."

"If I abandon Rosa Blanca, what are all my people to do? I'm responsible for their welfare. They belong here by natural laws, they're rooted like the trees in this soil. Removed from here, they'd wither, and their hearts and souls would be crippled. No, señor, I'm sorry, but I can't sell, simply because these families here have the same rights I have. What would they do? Where would they go? Where could they go? These people are part of the land they inhabit. What can they do once they've lost the ground that supported them? Answer me that, Señor Licenciado."

Pérez lit a cigarette, blew out the match and slowly crumbled the charred stick between his fingers. Then, suddenly, he made a face, as if he'd solved a tricky problem. He asked, naïvely, "What are these people to do? Well, the answer is simple. Si. They'll get good jobs at the oil camps."

Don Jacinto nodded vaguely, and said nothing.

Señor Pérez continued gazing at him, thinking of that man's Indian "stupidity," complaining to himself, "Why the devil didn't the Spaniards drown all these ox-headed Indians when they had the chance? To hell with it, it's high time to polish off this Rosa Blanca business, once and for all!"

≫ ≪

In Jacinto's slow process of thinking he had finally now arrived at the lawyer's proposition as to Rosa Blanca men working in Condor oilfields.

"It's true, lawyer, I've heard that men make big money in oil camps. José's boy who was born here now works at a camp. He's got to earn money, pronto, so's to get married. And his girl's father won't give consent until that boy gives him a cow as proof that he's a manly boy, a provider. Yes; then there's Marcos. He's worked at the camps, but he's back at Rosa Blanca. Says he'll never go back to the oil. Says a team of oxen can't drag him from here again. Says he was always unhappy there, and disgraced, the way they treated him. But he's happy here."

"Well, he must be a type of tonto, who doesn't know a good deal when he sees it. You've got to know the tricks to make money, and that's a plain fact. Nobody gives money away. You've got to work for it, Don Jacinto, or get it by other means."

"Perhaps, señor. But I wouldn't care to work in an oil camp."

"You'll never have to, Don Jacinto. You can buy yourself an automobile, a regular gas buggy that'll go ten times as fast as your best mule."

"No, thanks. I need no automobile," said Don Jacinto, without a spark of interest. "And, señor, if I had one I'd never use it, not ever."

Now Pérez felt as if he'd been kicked, and denied the

right to kick back. He racked his brains for a newer, better argument against Don Jacinto's total lack of money-sense. But before he found an idea that might penetrate that Indian hard skull, Jacinto at his own pace had come upon a good response to the lawyer's offer of well-paid jobs for all Rosa Blanca men. And it was more effective debating than Pérez could have expected from the simple Jacinto.

"You'd put the men and boys into the oil camps. Good. Magnificent of you. And I know these people would work hard and earn that big money. But there's one little bug in the cream. When the wells are all drilled, what about the jobs? Once the camps are set up and oil is being pumped into tank cars, what about those men who built the camps and rigged the derricks? What'll happen to all those men, Señor Pérez?"

"Condor drills many wells," retorted Pérez, as quickly as a lawyer can. "The Company occupies fields in various parts of the Republic. So, if the work ends here, the men will be sent to other camps, newer ones."

Jacinto, finding himself in view of the target, said calmly, "On those distant newer camps of which you speak, where our men will be sent, on those lands there must be workers who belong there, who sold their holdings to Condor Oil—well, señor. If our men are sent there, where will the displaced families go?"

Pérez felt trapped. Looking for a quick escape from this tricky Indian, he exploded, "Clearly, Don Jacinto, can't you see that those Indians there must go look for another place as soon as our men from here arrive there. . . ."

"Look, lawyer, as I see it, their holdings on which they lived and worked have been bought, leaving them homeless. Right? Now how can they earn a living if our men come along and take their jobs? Without land and jobs, they'll die. Besides, Señor Pérez, there's one other thing we haven't looked at: your oil wells can't last forever. They're bound to dry up some day, and by then men will have forgotten how to grow maize."

All problems are simple when enough land is available, and enough men on the soil who know how to cultivate it and love it; but all problems are complicated the moment men are displaced from the land to which they belong. Now, even law-yer-agent Pérez began to understand this. For the Indian had yanked him out of his solid position in his professional world. Yes, he had drawn him even from the region of opinions he'd studied in school and learned in life. Were another educated person seated opposite Pérez there, a merchant, a business-man, an architect, a banker, a city man in place of that Indian, Pérez would easily solve that problem. For Pérez had lived in the city, and knew city ways.

City men make short work of such problems, for they speak the same language, world over, hold the same views, and face the city's countless opportunities.

Yet despite all that they'd say, whatever remedies were discussed, the unanswered question was, "Where will we find land to cultivate?"

Even the lawyer would admit that city scientists were un-likely to invent ways of making corn from coal clinkers and beans from crude oil scums.

Jacinto's logic upon the knottiest problems of the human race were so simple and so clever that Licenciado Pérez felt lost. He couldn't touch the Indian with lessons in higher and lower economics, for it was plain that he and Jacinto lived in different worlds.

Jacinto didn't know that he'd licked the lawyer, because he didn't know how such men think; they in their world, he, Jacinto, by the earth and with the earth, rooted like a tree. Be-ing such, he couldn't be conquered by man's most impressive weapon, which Pérez had reserved during their talk.

Now, Pérez reached and brought up the white canvas bag which he'd put on the floor with his Stetson on top of it. Lifting it in both hands to make it appear even heavier than it was, and putting on his big public smile as if to say, "Now, my good man, get ready to see the world's wonders, and then some! The look of a lifetime!" Grunting, as if the money-bag weighed all that, he rose from the big chair, and said, "Will you please come along with me, Don Jacinto, and I'll show you something worth seeing."

Don Jacinto had risen, and they went through the always

open door into the large main hall with its high beamed ceiling and brick floor.

In the middle of the hall stood a massive mahogany table, built on Rosa Blanca maybe five hundred years ago. A few hand-tooled chairs were at the table, and some twenty stood along the walls, ready for the crowds of guests who often came to the hacienda. Now, in the quiet daytime, the table's surface gleamed clean and empty.

"Let's sit down and have a little talk, Don Jacinto," said Señor Pérez, smiling broadly, swinging the fat money-bag like a church bell, and managing to tinkle its coins. And as soon as Don Jacinto sat at the table, Pérez, dramatic as a magician, raised the money-bag high above the table center, seized the bottom seam, flipped the fat bag, and let the contents cascade upon the table. There it glittered, a heap of gold coins, each one a so-called azteca worth twenty pesos. The trick had been pulled off so cleverly that the strewn coins covered the table top and not one had rolled off onto the floor; perhaps it was chance, or perhaps the lawyer had practiced that trick a hundred times.

Pérez tenderly regarded the spread-eagled gold as if it were the body of a certain woman of his, his eyes caressing her breasts. He hovered there hypnotically, unable to turn away his eyes. Plainly, his mind was crowded with scores of desires, dozens of imagined objects that could be acquired with this little mountain of gold; how well he knew that each coin could purchase certain exquisite pleasures from certain creatures—if only the coins were his.

Brusquely, he broke his own trance, sighed loudly, and glanced from the sprawled-out gold to Jacinto, who hadn't budged nor blinked at the rich display on his homemade old table.

Staring at Don Jacinto, Pérez reddened. "Great God, I hope this man hasn't read my mind while I was skirting the world!" He shook his head, hoping to shake off such thoughts as he managed his business-as-usual smile. But this smile, too, happened to be a perfect copy of a New Year's Eve smile he'd turned onto his bedded mistress, years ago, when he'd lifted

that pillow to display a diamond bracelet, his first impressive
gift to her.

So he smiled, or leered, during his counting of these azteca coins, performing the count like a solemn rite, working
not only to impress Don Jacinto, but because he really believed the handling of gold to be the noblest work done by a
human being.

At last the counting was finished and the little columns
were lined up on that mahogany surface in ranks like golden
soldiers ready to be reviewed by a Secretary of War.

Reverently, with respect for the shining soldiers, and
without raising his eyes from them, he intoned, "There you
are, Don Jacinto, you're a rich man. Condor delivers you this
batch of gold in exchange for your Rosa Blanca. Four
hundred thousand pesos in gold aztecas, that's what Condor
pays you. Yes, it's real gold here before your eyes, so don't
think you're dreaming!"

But Pérez hadn't finished his mathematical magic. "As
you can see, Don Jacinto, this is only two hundred thousand
pesos, or just half of what you'll receive when the land deed is
signed, sealed, and stamped by the authorities. Understand,
you've got coming to you another heap of aztecas exactly like
this! Tomorrow, if you wish. Just say the word!—your word
is as good as gold, and I'll see to it that you get the gold. It's
waiting for you, Don Jacinto."

But the impression that Señor Pérez had hoped to make
on the Indian fell completely flat. Don Jacinto idly picked off
a coin, hefted it on his palms, examined its stamped edge,
bit it with his sharp teeth, and said calmly, "Handsome coins,
those. The man that made those must be a true artisan, in
order to fashion bits of metal so prettily." And he carefully
replaced the coin on the proper column.

That pile of gleaming coins signified less to him than a
little mountain of maize kernels or a carload of pigs, for all of
which he wouldn't trade Rosa Blanca—gold, corn, pigs—not
even with a bonus of some trainloads of horses. For Rosa
Blanca meant more to him than any collection of things.

He could bear it no longer standing by that table of
golden toys. His heart pounded, his spirit trembled in fear

and joy. In his eyes, the great hall was as dim as if swallowed in a cloud.

He arose, and went outdoors.

There he stood in the portico and gazed over the great patio. As always it wasn't very orderly, despite his orders that it be cleaned up daily and kept clean.

A hundred times he'd ordered those broken saddles to be taken out of there, and the bottomless baskets, too, and every time Don Jacinto saw them, he was reminded to have them removed, pronto. But each time there was nobody around to do it. Going for somebody, he came upon other chores, other problems, and so forgot the first one, which he remembered only on returning to the patio. And so things went, year after year, unchanged, as they had been for centuries.

In the farthest corner, leaning against the adobe wall that enclosed the patio and yard, lay an old wheel of an ancient carreta, no living person could recall. The wheel was dry and silvery with age, but it had been cunningly made from mountain oak, good for years yet, maybe a century, before the termites could eat it up. Now, every Saturday when the workers came for pay and orders, Don Jacinto told someone to please take that wheel out of there, among other odd things; but every Sunday morning when Don Jacinto stepped out into the portico, yawning at the sunrise and stretching his arms and legs to test their usefulness, and to learn, sure enough, that they were still strong and in working order, the first thing he'd see was that old cart wheel, and it seemed to wink at him, for it had won. It won its right to that corner, over and over. It was part of the patio, for the corner would look vacant without that wheel. All the same, he meant to tell José, or anyone at hand, on Saturday, to get that wheel the hell out of there, or he'd hear about it, hombre!

But the old wheel stayed. And now Don Jacinto was happy to see it, just as he'd seen it since he was a five-year-old, spinning it, pretending that it was part of a merry-go-round the circus had left behind, just for him. He recalled his father saying, "Don't you kids ruin that there wheel, it's still good and strong enough to be put to good use, and maybe I'll put it onto another carreta—humm—or I could maybe use it at the trapiche on the sugar mill. Sí. I'll talk it over with Manuel, in a day or so." And so the wheel stayed, waiting.

At nine, Jacinto and his pals had converted the carreta wheel into a complete gymnasium, by raising it upon blocks, where they twined their slim bodies like snakes and slithered through the spokes.

Years later, by now bored with being snakes or Indian braves, Jacinto and other teenagers stretched out on the huge wheel at nighttime, telling bloody yarns about battles and escapades in which the wheel might have been involved, carrying goods and silver in mining country where the carters fought fierce battles with savage Indians, with highwaymen, and murderers. And though the boys hardly believed their own yarns, although some of them proved to be true!, about that old wheel, the boys were afraid to pass near the wheel at midnight.

Jacinto now remembered the day he'd found the wheel a handy place to tie onto it a baby coyote he and his companions had caught in the nearby bush. Yes, Jacinto had the idea of training the captive coyote to be a fierce watchdog that would terrorize anyone trying to snoop around Casa Grande. A good idea, but the coyote had no idea of waiting at leash end to be a great watchdog, for he soon chewed the rawhide leash in two and took off to his insecure bushland which he seemed to prefer to the security of guarding a patio.

But the wheel stayed. At one time Manuel, the mayordomo, or someone had condemned the wheel to be cut into fuel for the kitchen womenfolk. But father Yañez had delayed the order, saying that the old wheel could be used for something somewhere, for it was certainly stronger than those new-fangled wheels that may roll along for awhile, only to break down under a big load, not like those good old wheels of bygone days! And yes, he'd take it, maybe, to the sugar mill.

So the wheel survived. And when Jacinto was about twenty, he sat on the wheel with his legs hanging from spokes to ground while he sang to himself in nighttime hours. Or he was lucky enough to murmur and sigh and dream with his girl Conchita, yes, she who was now his faithful wife of many years already. But then in those days he'd sit there on moon-light nights humming phrases, singing and whistling senti-mental old ranch songs and corridos loaded with eternal love, broken promises, and shattered hearts. And more than one night, with moonlight or without it, he was seated there alone and crying like a child, his pride humiliated by Con-chita, the one woman in his life who was meant to love him and marry him for better or for worse. Bueno, if she wouldn't marry him, he'd remain a bachelor, no matter that people re-garded him as the future ruler of Rosa Blanca, yes, it'd be her fault if he let his name die for the lack of a wife!

Then came the time of sweet memories, when Jacinto and Conchita as newlyweds had often met like lovers on the old wheel in moonlight, and he cut notches in the dry old wood with a knife or nail, and now he remembered his feeling of re-cording each notch for private reasons, imagining now that he could see and count them from across the patio.

In time father Yañez had passed on, and he, Jacinto, be-came fully responsible for Rosa Blanca. Others passed, but the wheel stayed. It hadn't been moved an inch from the spot it occupied when, long long ago, he'd pretended it was a part of an abandoned merry-go-round.

Manuel, the seventy-five-year-old foreman, soon fol-lowed his respected master Yañez to the eternal hunting grounds. Many times old Yañez and Manuel had discussed what in hell they ought to do with that sturdy old wheel, but there it rested to this day, surely not even knowing that Manuel and father Yañez might be spending part of their time in eternity still discussing what they ought to have done with it when they were on earth.

Yes, the wheel had survived all Saturday clean-ups, all the women's empty fuel bins in the kitchen corner, all the or-ders to "Get that damned old thing out of there," yes, and if orders had been obeyed and Don Jacinto had come out one Sunday to stretch into the sunrise and found no wheel to frown at, he'd have felt robbed, and he'd have ordered the men to find and put it back there!

But there it was, the old carreta wheel, peaceful, tena-cious, wise in its own proud value, dreaming over its long history, still firm in silvery gray wood, stoically awaiting the day when nature would be done with it.

Don Jacinto had seen his son, Domingo, seated on it while he dreamed open-eyed, oblivious of all about him, singing and whistling his songs. Too, Don Jacinto had seen him notching the spokes; and one night he'd found Domingo red-eyed, but Domingo had explained that he'd eaten too much of that green chili sauce, the kind that might cause red eyes! Don Jacinto knew who the girl was, he approved of the girl, and thought that Domingo had chosen wisely, regardless of the sauce that caused red eyes.

Now, whatever Domingo did, whoever the girl he'd choose, Don Jacinto was sure that the carreta wheel would stay in its patio corner to the day that he, Jacinto, should be called to go and meet his father and Manuel in the eternal hunting grounds. The wheel would stay. For it was not merely an inanimate object, not just a piece of patina-ed wood, but much more: a symbol.

A symbol of the race that peopled the Republic, a race that was and ever will be the same.

A race that can't be moved.

That outwits time, and endures.

➢ ➣

Beyond the low dividing wall in the great front patio, Don Jacinto saw his head foreman, Margarito, the mayor-domo of Rosa Blanca, doctoring a drove of mules that suffered pack saddle sores from carrying hacienda products over the steep mountain trails.

First, Margarito cleans the raw red sores with black soap and warm water, and then with a stick, covered with a rag soaked in a special tar salve he works deep into the wounds. This tar salve kills the grubs that burrow into the flesh. To some of the wounds, Margarito applies fine ashes of burnt leather, which promotes new skin in a few days. The mules submit to the doctoring while a boy holds them and Margarito sings while at his job.

Jacinto is Margarito's compadre and godfather of some of his children, while Margarito is godfather of Jacinto's two eldest children, Domingo and Juanita. Yet, everybody at Rosa Blanca knows that Margarito was more than just that, for without doubt Don Jacinto was Margarito's father. Margarito neither denied nor discussed this. His mother who was still living and busy with the hacienda's hen-house as well as general work at the Casa Grande, never said yes or no, for she was neither proud nor ashamed of what anyhow could be of no practical value to anybody.

Rosa Blanca never begrudged its flocks of children, those niños who were certainly born in love or they wouldn't have been born at all. Being alive, being there on Rosa Blanca they had the right to stay, and Don Jacinto naturally cared for them. He didn't need any Civil Court to order him to support orphans on the place. He carried the truest laws in his blood.

Indeed, such laws as are not founded in man's blood, in man's instinct for justice, are dead laws anyway.

Don Jacinto now turned to look at Rosa Blanca's own little village of workers' huts.

At this noon hour, all the huts and jacalitos were breathing smoke; it puffed up out of the ever-open doorways, from slits in the palm-thatched roofs, and from openings in the mud walls. The women worked outside near their own huts in the shade of the overhanging roof; they were shelling beans or grinding corn, their "nixtamal."

Turkeys, chickens, pigs, tame and wild birds, burros, dogs, cats, and maybe a raccoon or a monkey ran loose around the earthen patio in front of the huts, and came near when the women were grinding nixtamal, or clapping and patting tortillas between their palms. For the animals knew that morsels would fall, or bits of nixtamal dough be rubbed off the women's hands, and they waited for such bits.

It amused the women to pause, wipe sweat from their face, and fling a tidbit of dough or tortilla to the animals that appreciated it enough to snarl and fight over it, and pose for more. How the women laughed, sometimes to tears, to see a quick little monkey outwit a great clumsy dog, or a turkey snatch a morsel from a hen's very beak!

Laughing, mocking the animals, they bent to their work with renewed energy.

The grinding of nixtamal wasn't hard work. Their work was easier in never knowing that a machine could do it twenty times as fast. Besides, the hand-ground tortilla tasted better, for the delicate flavor of the stone-ground and hand-patted tortilla cannot be produced by any machine.

In the porch of a hut over there, Jacinto saw the rusty barrel hoop hung by a hemp string from the rafters, with one Loro, a wicked old parrot, at home in the hoop. A board was wired to the hoop with a clay water cup balanced on it; and the green-suited old parrot paced along this board with his glassy eyes glaring at the world around him. He wasn't tied there, but he knew a home when he saw it, and he stayed with it. He shuffled along the board heckling burros, cats, pigs, and dogs. Each afternoon when he received his two little tortillas, specially made for him, he pecked off a few bits for himself, and tore the rest into offerings, gifts, and bribes for chosen or would-be friends, be they dogs, burros, or pigs. He was known to use tidbits as bait for a free-for-all among the animals down under, this baronial Loro.

Lately, it seems that one of those little pigs was his preferred friend, and Loro held some of his choicest morsels until this little pig came along. The scraggly little pig would turn his gray eyes upwards as if Loro were his god, able to give him a whole world. And if an ordinary hog happened to grab the morsel that Loro had dropped for his pig, he cackled and screamed.

Frankly, Loro was the vilest of the vile, for he heard everything and imitated everybody, each one in turn. His crazy collection of curses and blasphemies could be heard in milpas and pastures a good quarter mile away; and when the wind carried Loro's tantrums to the Casa Grande kitchen, Conchita and her women had to hold their ears, that is, if their hands were free. Oh, that Loro, he's badder than anybody.

Now, Don Jacinto heard Loro's nasal scream, and he

smiled, for he liked the cynical bird, for Loro was a kind of
scandal sheet, and had let fly with many a choice village
secret, for everybody's amusement and nobody's personal
harm. But Loro's croaking voice came to Jacinto not as a
single sound among the thousands of the hacienda, but as a
note in the whole harmony: the bored mooing of cows standing in the shade of ancient trees, hogs grunting and snorting,
turkeys gobbling, geese gaggling, burros harshly braying, children yelling lustily and gaily, a dog barking suddenly to be
echoed by twenty other dogs, a baby crying for attention; and
the sweet clapping of female hands on tortillas, the patty-pat-
pat of life's bread.

Women chattered by their tiny open hearths, Margarito
cured his pack-mules and continued his corrido of the linda
muchachita Indita. The patio back gate was opened, its ancient hinges screaming for just one drop of oil; a child howled
mightily as mother gave him a tiny spanking for busting another earthen pot. A man in the field shouted for José to
come give him a hand, but pronto, hombre; and flies, bees,
birds, beetles, crickets, and frogs tuned up for the day's finale
in the green swampy woods that rustled with wind. All these
sounds ebbed and flowed softly, all parts of a logical perma-
nence in the sun-shafted air around Don Jacinto, a music
sweeter than any orchestra ever invented by man, for this was
the eternal song of a hacienda in the tropics, in this case Rosa
Blanca's own inimitable voice, unlike any other sound upon
this earth.

Jacinto saw women coming toward the huts from the
river with the great clay water pots on their heads. Walking
sedately, raising a hand to just touch the balanced pot at
times, they moved so erectly, so dignified and queenly with
those heavy clay crowns on their heads, it wasn't possible to
imagine them bowing, except maybe to the Santísima. They
brought the water from the river in those vessels as brown as
their skins. Their bare feet clasped the earth. The water vessels they carried on their heads made them seem very tall; and
their long black hair, freshly washed in the river, hung loosely
down their backs, swaying to the slow rhythm of their walking.

And now the men were straggling home from the fields, orchards and pastures, ready for their meals and some rest. They walked loosely, in no hurry; some carried machetes, others mattocks; a few of them smoked a thick cigarette made of tobacco rolled in tender corn husks; some of them whistled or hummed or sang. The field boys horsed around, laughing, shouting, throwing chips or clods at each other.

Passing the little chapel near Casa Grande, they noticed its simple door decorated with fresh flowers from field, bush, and jungle. Upon the chapel's earthen floor was a thick soft carpeting of leaves and branches cut only a few hours earlier.

And so, this way Don Jacinto watched and meditated from the portico where he stood. And he saw Rosa Blanca's life as he'd seldom perceived it before. Never had he felt so deeply satisfied in being not the boss, not the ruler here, but something by far better: the center, the core, yes, the live heart of Rosa Blanca.

Deeply in his soul and in his mind he realized that if he abandoned Rosa Blanca it would collapse. Families would separate, ancestral ties would be broken. Sons would forget fathers, nephews their uncles. Rosa Blanca would cease to be the homeland of its people; and the scattered, disinherited sons would remember it only as a ranch, one of the hundreds that had been obliterated in the Republic.

Yes, the young would recall it as one more ranch from which they had moved with a pack of belongings on their backs, climbing over the mountains to find work at another oilfield, another mine, another factory. They would confuse Rosa Blanca with other places where their fathers had worked to earn bread; for, in the life ahead, their fathers would be moving from camp to camp in search of new work, more bread, more pesos to pay the way toward other camps, other jobs, without the least chance to own a piece of good earth under their sandals, without the security their forefathers had taken for granted.

In the migrant life of job-jumping, good pay. That is, one day, good pay. Thanks. Overtime, hurrah. Next day, half pay. Next week, nothing. Thanks. Sorry. And so they'd go

from camp to camp, from oilfield to oilfield, from one "pro-
gressive" project to another project, hoping to progress to a
few weeks of security, which of course wouldn't last. For
progress doesn't stay in one spot. It goes on. And those with
the calloused hands and bent backs, they'd stumble after it,
just as they were expected to do.

Jacinto knew little of all these things, but he sensed
them. His world was Rosa Blanca and the bush around it, the
wagon track road to Tuxpan and Tuxpan itself. He was in his
Indian world. But he did know for certain that if his people
were torn from heir paternal soil, something horrible would
happen to them.

He couldn't describe this horror, which he somewhat
imagined as the gasping hell of a fish yanked out of water to
struggle upon the sharp, hot sand; or, as a proud young tree
suddenly uprooted and dragged away with its moist tendrils
burnt to death under the broiling sun.

≥ ≤

To think of a solution to this problem so suddenly thrust
upon him, wasn't legally necessary to Don Jacinto, for he
could do as he pleased, as even Licenciado Pérez insisted.
Why should he worry about the problems? Not one of Rosa
Blanca's people would blame Jacinto if he did sell out, for
they accepted his word as law and expected him to act on his
own judgment, as indeed he must.

Pondering on all angles of his big problem, Jacinto recalled other rancheros and "hacendados" who had faced this
same issue. And he knew from their troubled experiences that
if a powerful foreign company once decides to acquire a par-
cel of land, it is almost impossible for a native to defend his
rights and retain his ancestral home.

Though these vast ranches are rich in land and produce,
they are not rich in dollar assets, for their life is built on intimate sustenance from the soil, in a barter-type economy. Not
one of these haciendas could raise the dollars to hire lawyers
to compete with the highly paid and highly favored lawyers

of a multi-million dollar corporation. Lawyers? Don Jacinto had never dealt with one until Condor had sicked the agent-lawyers onto him.

But there was a force even larger than dollar force that pressed on Don Jacinto from every side, and that was his own government. No native landowner or trustee of land, regardless of his race or citizen standing, could fight his own government, that insists he sell his ranch for the larger benefit of the public. The big men loom over the little rancher, "Listen, farmer, we're offering you more than your land is worth. Sell! Period. Punto." The public needs oil, they say, and what's more, the government needs the revenue from petroleum products. Sell, and be quick about it.

The quicker the oil is flowing and the more of it that is flowing, the quicker the income for the government. Aligned on the government side of the struggle are state governors, treasurers, generals, senators, congressmen, bankers, and corporation lawyers, all of whom have a hand in the business, the business of helping the poor little forty-million-dollar corporation defeat the great big Indian rancher who has all of a thousand pesos in the bank or buried in the back patio. Maybe he has. All of these forces pressing in on every side of the little rancher are called "advisers" to the government, and most of them are well paid for their "advice," which, oddly enough, favors the foreign corporations, and rarely the natives, because el dictador, el Caudillo, has to protect the myth of the Golden Era.

Sensing all this, Don Jacinto knew that he never could satisfy all parties to his terrible problem.

Jacinto stirred himself from his troubled day-dreams and called to Margarito who was still doctoring the pack-mules and singing the 60th stanza of the corrido leaving only about 60 more stanzas to go.

"Listen, compadre," Jacinto called. "Ven acá. Come here one momentito only."

"Sí, compadre, what's up? Something wrong?" asked Margarito, sauntering toward Jacinto, still humming the corrido.

Jacinto stood up there in the portico, and Margarito down

in the patio, with his arms resting lazily on the wooden rail. Jacinto jerked his head toward the sala, where Pérez was still guarding his golden "soldiers" so they wouldn't march off, never to return.

"That caballero in the sala is on the look-out for workers. Seems the oil camps need men. How about it compadre? Like to take a good job?"

"Me? What are you trying to say, compadre? You want me out of here? And who in hell'd be the mayordomo if I leave? Just tell me that, first."

"Don't worry, compadre. If we have to, we can do without you."

Margarito hesitated a moment, bending his head along his right shoulder and squinting at Jacinto. Something wrong with this deal, he thought. Then, "So? How much does that gent pay? I mean the señor in the sala."

"Four pesos a day."

"A day!" Margarito had doubt written all over his face. "Four pesos a day!—can't be. Never heard of hombres getting four pesos a day for bending their backs in common labor. A learned guy, maybe. But a laborer, oh no!"

"You listen to me. It's a sure thing. Absolutely. Four pesos a day. And maybe more, for overtime work."

"Dios mio, but that's a mountain of money! Caramba. Never thought I'd live to see four pesos for a day's work. Mmmm. How many days' work has the señor got, at four pesos a day?"

"As many as you want. Months and months. Years. Or so I figure from what he says."

"Years! That's too much for me. But if it seems to you, compadre, that I ought to go and take a four-peso a day job, why I'll do it, just for you, compadre. Yeah, I can go and work out there if I have to. But tell the gent that I only want four months' worth, at four pesos a day. Hombre! That's enough for me, Jacinto. Not a day more, and in three months I'll be back here with a load of pesos!"

"That's out, Margarito. You can't come back. Once you go, you go to stay," and Jacinto looked sharply at him.

"What's that? Repeat that, please, compadre. That I can't come back to Rosa Blanca? To my own home? Por que no?" Margarito couldn't grasp such an idea, for his door was always open, he'd come and gone as master of his hut, as foreman of the hacienda. Why not?

"It's simple enough, compadre," Jacinto tried to explain. "Simply that the caballero doesn't hire men who don't want to stick with the Company. You got to sign up for a long time, so as to be an experienced man, so the Company doesn't have to train new men all the time," Jacinto reasoned. Actually, Pérez hadn't told him this, but Jacinto thought big companies wanted permanent men; and besides, he wanted to find out how Margarito felt about permanent separation from Rosa Blanca. "See, Margarito, it's a big deal. Lots of oilfields. When the work slacks off at one field, the men are ordered to another field where they go to the same kind of work and get paid by the same Company. So you got to stick to the Company."

"But . . . but, caramba! Didn't Marcos come back? Sure he did. But you say that was another company, huh? And this Company doesn't want me to come back? Never?" Margarito mumbled this hard lesson to himself, but he couldn't understand it. He yelled angrily, "No, compadre! I prefer not to go. And I'm gonna forget them four pesos a day. What's four pesos? I mean, it's a lot here, but them prices go sky-high at the oil camps like Marcos was tellin' us." He wiped the sweat from his brown face and continued. "Hombre, how I could use them four pesos a day right now, what with two of my girls about to get hooked with a couple of lads who can't hardly scare up a dozen goats altogether. They got nothin' but the hut I'll have to show them how to build or build it myself. That's how it is with some of these young ones, these days. But pesos or no pesos, I ain't leavin' here if I can't come back.

Jacinto looked keenly at him, but said nothing. Margarito continued. "Marcos, he said them camps stink worse than all the pig pens from here to Tuxpan. And how the men fight, says Marcos. Quarrels, day and night. Bosses booting the men right and left. A foreman socks an Indito right in the mug and claims the Indito insulted him. And if you complain they beat you up for fair. Says the men are marched around with great pipes and tubes resting on the shoulders of twenty men marching along like they were chained to the pipes like slaves in chains. Says everybody is smeared with greasy crap and soaked with thick oil. Says the men are too tired to do anything but snarl at each other. A hell of a life for four pesos a day! No, compadre, you just go and tell that gent in there that it's not for me. No thanks. And that includes all my men. Tell him my men don't budge from here if they can't come back! And come to think of it, why don't that gent go and get workers from the big city? I hear tell that thousands of men are out of work in them big cities. No men out of work here at Rosa Blanca, and he won't get none of my men. You tell him, compadre. I've said my say."

"Remember, Margarito, three of our boys went to oil camps."

"I'll say I remember. First, Marcos came back. Next José's boy has got to stay at the camp to earn that cow for the boda so's his girl's father will let him have her. Last, there's Pedro's boy, he can't come back."

"Margarito, what's this? Pedro's boy can't come back?"

"Well, compadre, you don't know about that ruckus, because they're ashamed to tell you about it, but that boy went bad at the camps. He came around here, swearing worse than Loro. Yeah, he let fly with a few choice stinkers that made his mother blush, and that ain't easy. That was way back in Holy Week, of all times, and papa Pedro just told that nasty little Pete not to come back home no more, until he grows up, and that's gonna be a while. It seems that Pete is laced into a 'night-club' girl, compadre, if you know the kind I mean. Yeah, that kind. And Pete, more the idiot he, he'd marry that girl. So there he is, at the camps.

"Well, like you say, compadre, four pesos a day is really something to stop the river. But now I think of it, Marcos was tellin' how it all stinks, all around, and it's all noise and yelling and cursin' and no birds. And no sleepin' at night for the motor drills and pumps and trucks. To hell with it, I say."

And off he walked, singing the corrido. Now the mules were kicking and biting each other. "Hey, macho! Whoooa, you stinking coyote-face, you! Whoooa! Or I'll kick you so hard you'll think Christmas and Easter have fallen on the same day!" But Margarito's bark had no bite, for he separated the bored and feuding animals, and calmed them before continuing his doctoring. And his corrido.

Don Jacinto watched him, and he knew how right he was, and how wrong it would be to sell Rosa Blanca and commit families to oil camps. As Margarito thought, so would all the men here. Rosa Blanca belonged to all of them, for all of them had made it what it was.

$$\geqslant \leqslant$$

Returning to the sala, Don Jacinto found Licenciado Pérez still sitting at the table, gazing as if hypnotized at the golden columns. He wouldn't have risked leaving this fortune and joining Don Jacinto in the portico, oh no.

Actually, he could have left the gold there for a day, a week, or a month, and returned to find it untouched, not even one coin scraped or shaved down for whatever gold shavings are worth. Being a lawyer, he trusted no one, not even his own mother with any part of anything like this fortune on the table.

"Well, Don Jacinto, it's all added up and it's all settled now. We can all be glad that good old Rosa Blanca is sold at last! Believe you me, it cost me plenty of time and labor to convince you to do what's best for you, my good man."

Jacinto stood there, his face stern as he said, calmly, "Rosa Blanca is not sold, and Rosa Blanca never will be sold. Not even if you put ten times as much gold as you have there on that table. That gold means nothing to me, it's valueless for me. As I said once, I repeat, land can never be exchanged for money. Soil is soil, and money is money. They're two distinct and different things, like a tree above a stone."

Señor Pérez stood amazed. He gasped, "Rosa Blanca, not sold? You don't want all that money?"

"Not sold. You heard me, Señor Licenciado."

"I don't understand. You must be crazy to talk like this about soil and money. Every bit of land on earth is, was, or will be exchanged for money some day." Pérez said this so as to be saying something, but once spoken, the words sounded suspect even to his legal ears.

Jacinto stood there, a hard expression on his face. "No, Señor Licenciado, land and money cannot be interchanged. Soil is eternal as long as humans remain on this earth. Gold isn't eternal. It may change its value at any time, but soil never will. That's why you cannot buy this soil with your gold." His words rang out in the great silent sala.

"All right," said Pérez, wearily. "Agreed. Not sold, then." And he irately began sweeping the gold into the canvas money bag, handling it like fistfuls of sand, saying, with disgust, "Want to know what I really think of you, Jacinto? You're a stupid, half-crazy old idiot, and a disgraceful, monstrous imbecile. Men like you ought not to be allowed to exist, being a permanent danger to human society. We'll get Rosa Blanca yet! Don't worry, we'll get it somehow, believe you me. And what's more, we'll get it for less, much less, than we offered to pay you. Don't doubt the word of an experienced lawyer. We'll get it cheaper, and we'll get you, too, dead or alive. So don't say that I didn't warn you!"

"You can't scare me, Señor Pérez, neither you nor your stinking disreputable oil company!" Don Jacinto had somewhat deserted his usual stoic poise, and he spoke more angrily and roughly than he ever had spoken.

He snapped his fingers in the lawyer's face, and then grinned, just as readily as he'd been angered. "Well, lawyer, how about a shot of our genuine mezcal añejo before you head home? Here we are, Señor Licenciado."

And he brought the old bottle, filled two water glasses and they each took one. Jacinto lifted his glass to the height of his guest's eyes, and said heartily, "Salud!"

"Salud!" said the lawyer in the same way. And they both took the hard drink without stopping. Then each reached for a pinch of salt mixed with powdered toasted maguey worms, and sucked a slice of lemon as chaser.

"Doesn't that one deserve another, Señor Pérez?" said Jacinto, laughing good-naturedly.

"Right! Let him join his brother," replied the lawyer, laughing, warmed by the powerful drink.

Salud! Salud! Down went another round, like a ceremony.

Now the lawyer was tying up the money-bag, but he stopped, and looked right at Jacinto; "Are you absolutely sure, Don Jacinto, positively sure, that you won't say yes, and sell the place?"

"Absolutely sure," Jacinto said shortly, his tone indicating that this would be the last word on the affair.

The lawyer shrugged, tied the bag tightly, called for his attendant mozo to bring the horses. And he took leave with all the courtesies and formalities never omitted by a true caballero, even though he left as a frustrated man. Mounted, he turned to Don Jacinto who had seen him to the patio portal, and he nodded smiling, "Adiós, Don Jacinto; thanks for your hospitality—until we meet!" He shoved his gun around from his hip, spurred his horse, and away he went, followed by his mozo.

Jacinto walked slowly down the portico toward the kitchen entrance.

"Conchita! Please come here a minute!"

"Flying!" she cried out. And here she came, drying her hands on a towel. "What is it, Chinto? Has he gone, the señor? I thought he'd stay for supper, and perhaps also overnight."

"No. He had to get back to the city. He'll likely stay overnight at one of the villages along the way." Jacinto looked his wife straight in the eyes, "Conchita, what do you think of me?"

"What do you mean to say, Chinto? I don't understand."

"Look at me, take a good look at me."

Looking at his face, cocking her head from right to left and up and down in a comical way she said, "I don't see anything particular about you. You appear to me as you always do, but maybe a bit worried, that's all."

"Honestly, you don't think me crazy, Conchita?"

She burst out laughing. "So that's what bothers you! Crazy, good Lord, what nonsense. If you're crazy, then all of us are, and I especially. Who put such a crazy idea into your head! Watch out, you might be judged crazy if you think you are! I've never seen a man saner in mind and sounder in body than you are, Jacinto Yañez. And you called me in for this, me with my hands full of work? You may be a bit crazy at that, for asking such a question! Crazy, crazy? Whoever heard such nonsense?" she mumbled, already on her way back to the kitchen.

The Story of a Bomb

The Indian peasant, Eliseo Gallardo, had three pretty daughters all of marriageable age, the eldest sixteen, the youngest thirteen.

One day, Eliseo had a visit from Natalio Salvatorres, a young bachelor who had worked for several weeks in the nearby bush. From the wages he had made as a charcoal burner, Natalio had saved about fifty pesos. But after he had bought himself a new cotton shirt, cotton pants, a bast hat, and had paid for his board and lodgings, he had little left.

The Saturday before, at a dance in the village, Natalio had seen the three pretty Gallardo girls. But he had been able to dance only once with each, because the other young men had always been quicker and more determined than he. Natalio was a young man who needed time to make up his mind.

He spent all of the next day, Sunday, thinking things over. Finally, he arrived at a more definite idea, and spent Monday, Tuesday, and Wednesday getting better acquainted with it.

On Thursday his idea had matured enough so that by Friday he clearly knew what he wanted.

That is why he went on Saturday to see Eliseo, father of the three pretty daughters.

"Well, young man," Eliseo asked, "which one of the three do you want?"

"That one," said Natalio, and nodded his head toward Sabina, the daughter who was fourteen and had the prettiest bosom of the three.

"That's what I thought," Eliseo said. "She would suit you very fine. You're not so dumb. By the way—what is your distinguished name?"

After Natalio had given his full name, which he could pronounce but could not write or spell, the girl's father asked how much money he had.

"Twenty pesos," Natalio said. This was twice as much as he really had.

"Then you cannot have Sabina," said Señor Gallardo. "I need a new pair of pants, and my old woman has no shoes at all. If you want to aim so high as to ask for Sabina, you can't expect her mother and father to run about in dirty rags. What do you think our standing is in the village anyway? There must be new pants for me and at least one pair of white or brown canvas shoes for the woman. Otherwise, there's no place for you in my family. Let me have some of your tobacco."

After the cigarettes had been rolled and lighted, Natalio said, "Bueno, Don Eliseo, I'll be satisfied also with as fine a girl as that one over there." This time he nodded toward Filomena, eldest of the three.

"You are smart, muy listo, Natalio. Where are you working?"

"I own a burro—and a good young donkey it is, too."

"No horse?"

These questions about his financial situation made Natalio very uneasy. He spit several times on the earthen floor of the hut before he spoke again.

"I have an uncle who works in a mine up near Parral," he said. "More than a hundred mines are up there. As soon as I have a woman, I'll be on my way there to work. My uncle will see to it that I get a job. He is very friendly with one of the most important foremen."

"Ah, yes," Eliseo said.

"And what do you think, Don Eliseo? One can easily make three pesos a day in those mines."

"Three pesos a day is good money," Eliseo said. "But that pitiful twenty pesos you have right now is nothing to brag about. With so little money, we can't even make a wedding."

"Why not?" Natalio asked. "A wedding can't cost so much. A minister? Well, we surely can't pay him—so we'll have to do without the help of the church. And as for a marriage license—we can't pay for that either, can we?"

"You're right, Natalio," Eliseo said. "There's not enough money in the whole world to pay for such things. And besides, they have little to do with a wedding anyway."

"Very little indeed," Natalio said.

"Of course," said Eliseo, "we must have at least two musicians for the dance. Then there must be three bottles of mezcal—or better still, four. Otherwise people here in the village might talk. They might say that Filomena was not married to you at all and had only run off with you like a hussy. I tell you, muchacho, things are not done that way in my family. Not *my* daughters—no, señor. We are honest people. Don't think one of my daughters would run away with you without permission. You could wait a thousand years for such a thing to happen in my family. Not with a father like me around. No, señor—not in this family."

The two men continued negotiating for another two hours, drinking many cups of coffee and smoking most of Natalio's tobacco. In the end they agreed that Natalio should go back to the bush until he had earned enough money to pay for the musicians, the bottles of mezcal, two pounds of coffee, six pounds of brown sugar, one pair of light canvas shoes for the girls' mother, and one pair of pants for the father. In addition, Eliseo pointed out, there should be two pesos for sweet bread to be eaten with the coffee by the women and children who came to the wedding. In fact, Eliseo said, the whole village would be at the wedding, and if a few pesos happened to be left over for unexpected guests from a neighboring village, so much the better for the family's good name.

When the deal was closed, and Natalio had accepted all of Eliseo's conditions, he was told that he would be permitted to lodge and board with the family. He would have to pay for this, of course—but the cost would be one-third less than he was paying now. He was to occupy a certain corner of the family's one-room adobe hut, but—since there might be difficulties and annoyances if it were handled otherwise—Filomena was to be permitted to sleep in that same corner, provided Natalio would buy her a new blanket.

Natalio agreed, and hurried to the nearest general store where he bought a new blanket in the brightest colors he could find. Then he bought a bottle of mezcal to celebrate the deal, and returned to the hut.

All the members of the family, including Filomena herself, had been present the whole time the two men had been negotiating what, to them, was a straightforward business matter.

After everyone had taken a drink from the bottle of mezcal, Filomena was asked by her father if she had something to say.

"I'd like very much to go to Parral," she said.

Natalio was short those ten pesos he had claimed to have in his pocket; and during the eight weeks he worked in the bush his new shirt and pants went to pieces, in spite of the fact that he was very careful with them. He had to buy a new shirt and a new pair of pants for the wedding, and it was because of this that an American farmer, who had a ranch only a few miles from the village, discovered one day that two of his best cows were missing.

The wedding dance was over. Señor Gallardo had been quite drunk, but not too drunk to take great care not to get mud on his new yellow cotton pants. His wife had worn her new brown canvas shoes during only the first hour of the party. Then she had wrapped them in paper, replaced them in the cardboard box in which they had been sold, and hidden them so well that none of her daughters could find them.

Because everything had taken place just the way it had been planned beforehand, Filomena was now Natalio's esposa, respected by everybody as a wife whom nobody must take away or lead astray.

Natalio loaded his two blankets, a coffee kettle, a small bast bag containing provisions, his machete, his ax, and his Filomena on his burro and started off for the mines.

He had no uncle there. This had been another of his various lies to win the confidence of Filomena's father. Nevertheless, because he was willing to take any job, no matter how hard it might be, it was less than a week before he found work. He did not make three pesos a day, of course; all he earned was one peso seventy-five.

During his spare time, Natalio built a flimsy adobe hut, much like all the others in the village. Here he and Filomena led the life of the average Indian miner and his wife. She cooked his meals, did his laundry, patched his shirt and pants, picked the sandfleas out of his feet, and warmed up his bed in the cold nights so frequent in mountain regions.

He was very happy, Natalio was; he never got drunk. And Filomena, obviously, had no cause for complaint. This status quo might have lasted for a whole lifetime, had it not been for a young miner who discovered in Filomena something special and wonderful—something Natalio would never even have suspected she possessed.

And so it happened that when Natalio came home from work one night, he found no wife in his nest. And as she had taken with her the beautiful blanket, her extra undershirt, the three muslin dresses, and her comb—all the things he had bought her—he knew she had left for good.

The huts in the village were so carelessly made, and built of such poor material, that they were in no condition to keep secret anything that happened under their roofs. They had no windows, and because of this the doors were always left open until the inhabitants retired for the night.

It was, therefore, not difficult for Natalio to find the hut he was looking for. He could hear his Filomena laughing and chattering. Through the walls of this particular hut, made of a light network of twigs and sticks, Natalio spied Filomena sitting happily at the side of her newly chosen one. She was in excellent spirits. She and her new man were having a much more joyful time than any Natalio had ever had with her. She had never looked at him or caressed him in the way she was now favoring her lover.

Two other young couples were in the hut. And although there was much talk and laughter, Natalio did not hear his name mentioned even once. The way his existence was ignored, he might as well have been dead a long time.

It is a foolish undertaking to seek to determine the true motives for an action performed by a member of a race not our own. Perhaps we find the motive—or we might believe that we have found it—but when we attempt to understand it, to reconcile it with our own attitudes toward the world and our own souls, we are in as hopeless a position—assuming that we are honest enough to admit it—as if we tried to decipher unknown stone symbols carved by a long-vanished people. Members of the Caucasian race will always be unjust when placed in the position of judges of the actions of members of other races.

What Natalio did now can be communicated solely in terms of his actions and their consequences. To give an explanation of his actions would necessitate a study that would fill a thick book.

When Natalio had convinced himself that Filomena was now far too happy and too much in love to ever think of returning to him, he decided to bring this episode of his life to an end.

He went to the barn where explosives were kept, crawled under the sheet-iron wall, and stole some dynamite and a fuse.

Back in his own hut, Natalio worked steadily and patiently. With the skill and intelligence inherent in Mexican Indians, he constructed in a surprisingly short time, and from the crudest imaginable materials, an excellent bomb, using as a bombcase an empty tin can he had found near the general store.

As soon as he finished the bomb, Natalio crept again to the hut where he had found Filomena with her lover. The three couples were still there, and even more animated and jolly than before. Filomena's lover was playing a mouth organ, with Filomena cuddled up against him, and by all appearances the three couples intended to keep the party going until the men had to go to work again in the morning.

It was easy for Natalio to throw the lighted bomb through the open door into the hut.

This done, he went back to his own hut and lay down to sleep, content with the knowledge that he had made the most effective bomb of which he was capable. The outcome was of no special interest to him. Should the bomb go off, as he was sure it would, everything would be all right; if it didn't everything would be all right too. After the bomb had been completed and properly delivered to the right place, the whole matter of his marriage had lost all interest for him. As to what might happen afterward—he left that to providence. From now on—and for all time to come—Filomena and her new man would be safe from him. For Natalio, this episode was closed forever.

But not so for the three laughing couples inside the hut. . . .

In the mining districts, every Indian, man and woman alike, knows what it means to see at one's feet an old tin can to which a smoking fuse is attached.

The occupants of the hut saw the bomb and dashed out of the hut without even taking time for a shout of horror. This took them less than half a second. At once a terrific explosion followed, sending the hut up a hundred feet into the air.

Of the six people who had been inside, five escaped without so much as a scratch. The sixth, the young woman of the couple that owned the hut, was not so fortunate.

This woman had, at the very moment the bomb made its appearance at the party, been busy making fresh coffee in the corner of the hut farthest from the door. She had neither seen the bomb nor noted the rapid and speechless departure of her guests. Consequently, she accompanied the hut on its trip upward. And since she had been unable in so short a time to decide which part of the hut she would like best to travel with, she landed at twenty different places in the vicinity.

Two days later a police agent came to the mine to see Natalio and ask him what he might know about the explosion. The agent questioned Natalio at the place where he was working, in an open excavation, but Natalio did not allow himself to be seriously interrupted. Only when he paused to wipe the sweat from his face and roll a cigarette, did he honor the agent with answers to his questions.

"You threw the bomb into the choza of Alejo Crespo, didn't you?" the agent asked.

"That's right," Natalio said. "But it's none of your business. It's purely a family affair."

"A woman was killed by that bomb."

"I know it. You don't have to tell me. It's my woman, and I can do with her whatever I wish, for she gets from me her meals, and all her clothes, and I paid for the music at the wedding. There are no debts left. Everything is paid."

Natalio knew what he was talking about. There was no nonsense in what he said, and he was telling nothing but the truth.

"But the trouble is," the agent said, "it wasn't your woman who was killed. It was the Crespo woman."

"So? If it was the Crespo woman that was killed, then I've nothing to do with it whatever. I don't know her. The Crespo woman has never done me any harm. If she was killed, it was most certainly not my intention. In such case it was just an accident. And I am not responsible for accidents. The Crespo woman is a grown-up woman who can look out for herself, and she doesn't need me to protect her. If she'd taken better care of herself, this wouldn't have happened to her. I'm not her guardian, and not her man either, and I don't give a damn for women who don't take care of their health."

With that, the matter was taken care of as far as Natalio was concerned. He threw his cigarette stub away, lifted his pickax, and struck furiously at the rocks, indicating he had important work to do and could not waste his time with idle talk which was of no interest to him.

Six weeks later, the case came up for trial. Natalio was charged with murder, though no degree was mentioned. The jury consisted of Indians like himself. Two were foremen at the mines, one was a carpenter, one a butcher, another a baker, others were storekeepers and saloonkeepers. None of them had even the slightest interest in Natalio's conviction. All of them depended on miners remaining at work, because no money could be made from miners in jail.

Natalio's friends had advised him to keep his mouth shut as much as possible. If he was forced to answer any questions, they told him, he should say absolutely nothing other than, "I don't know."

This advice suited Natalio quite well. He disliked working with his head, and simply answering, "I don't know," required no work at all.

He was not deeply concerned about the outcome of his trial. If he was convicted and had to go to prison—or even if he was sentenced to be shot—it would be all right with him. On the other hand, if he was acquitted, he would go back to his work, which he liked immensely.

He rolled a cigarette, showing no emotion whatever. He cared nothing at all about the trial preparations going on about him in the crumbling adobe town hall.

Finally, the stage was set. Everybody in the courtroom smoked cigarettes, including the judge, the public prosecutor, the gentlemen of the jury, and the half-dozen or so miners. These visitors had come, not because of any real interest in the trial, but because they were not working, due to injuries received in the mines, and had no other place to while away their time. They would have preferred to hang around the bars but they had no money. Some of them had bandages on their face or head, others carried their arms in slings, and one had crutches leaning against his leg.

The public prosecutor stood up. "The defendant has made a full confession," he said. "The police officer who questioned him only two days after the crime was committed is present to be called to the witness stand, should it so please your Honor and the honorable gentlemen of the jury."

The prosecutor was sure he had a clear-cut case and would have no trouble getting a conviction. What really concerned him, however, was the chance that he might not be able to catch the train in time to return to town, which would mean spending the night in this miserable, stinking little village.

The men on the jury had begun to dislike the prosecutor. They resented his arrogance and the way he showed how he detested the people of the village, especially the miners, and they had seen how much he hated to have been ordered to a place where he could not walk half a block without losing his shoes in the mud.

Because they wanted to see the overbearing prosecutor miss his train and go home defeated by the men he despised, the jurors insisted on their right to question both defendant and witnesses, if they thought it was necessary in order to clear up the case for their better understanding. If Natalio himself should benefit by this procedure, so much the better. The men on the jury were much impressed by Natalio because he was so calm and stoic.

The judge welcomed these unusual interruptions by the gentlemen of the jury. He had to stay overnight anyway, because he had several other cases to attend to. These interruptions made the trial less dull for him and shortened his day. He was thankful for this, because Natalio's was the only case for the day, and he had nothing to do with his time once it was over. He usually slept the time away in places like this, but he had already slept so much here that he was tired of it.

One of the jurors asked the judge to please ask the defendant if it was true that he had confessed to the murder.

Natalio rose clumsily. "I don't know, señor," he said. He sat down again and replaced his cigarette between his lips.

Another juror asked to see the written statement of Natalio's confession.

The prosecutor jumped to his feet. "This statement, gentlemen of the jury, is written and signed by the police officer, which was necessary because the defendant can neither read nor write. In due time I'll call the officer to testify here in court. The witness is an honorable and reliable police officer with an excellent record and many years of service. We have no reason whatever to question his written and verbal statements, nor the results of his careful investigation of this case." He bent down over his little table and began fingering his papers with obvious uneasiness.

Another member of the jury wanted to know why he and his honorable colleagues should be obliged to believe more in the word of a policeman, who received his salary from the taxpayers' money, than in the word of an honest and sober miner like Natalio, who did not live, and never had lived, on the money of the taxpaying citizens. He said it was well known that Natalio worked hard for his living and that he produced valuable goods for the benefit of the whole nation.

Still another juror asked the defendant to confess right then and there, in the very face of the jury, that he had committed the crime he was charged with.

The judge called upon Natalio. "You heard what the honorable gentleman of the jury wishes to know. Did you kill the Crespo woman?"

Natalio rose only halfway. "I don't know, señor," he said quietly, and began to roll another cigarette.

The prosecutor jumped to his feet. "But you did throw the bomb, didn't you, Natalio?" he demanded. "Tell us the truth, my man! Lying won't help you. You did throw the bomb!"

With a bored note in his voice, Natalio said, "I don't know nothing." He sat down again and puffed away at his cigarette with signs of an undisturbed conscience.

The prosecutor did not call the policeman, as he had said he was going to do. He knew they would ask the policeman if it was not true that he received his salary from the taxes paid by the citizens. As soon as the policeman admitted it was so, the jury would then ask the prosecutor where *his* salary was coming from. And this, the prosecutor realized, would lead to still another question. The jury would ask, quite seriously, whether—inasmuch as both the policeman and the prosecutor received their salaries from the same source and therefore served the same boss—there might not exist a certain connection with the object of convicting an honest miner for no other purpose than to justify the necessity of their respective offices.

Because he foresaw such a layman's distortion of the facts the prosecutor decided against calling the policeman to the stand. Instead, he called Filomena, together with the others who were present in the hut when the bomb was thrown. Inasmuch as these witnesses belonged to the mining community, their testimony would be so solid that even the most spiteful members of the jury would have to accept it without question. The prosecutor considered Filomena his star witness. He was sure she would tell the truth, because she certainly knew the bomb had been intended for her, and she would feel much safer knowing that Natalio was in prison for several years.

Filomena and the other witnesses knew perfectly well what the whole community knew: that is, that nobody else but Natalio had been the maker and thrower of the bomb. Natalio had left no one in the village with any doubt as to who it was who knew how to defend his honor and how to punish an unfaithful wife.

But the prosecutor had had little experience with Indian mining folk such as these, and he by no means fully understood them.

He did not know that these mountain people would not, under any circumstances, bear witness against one of their own in a case such as this one. These mountain Indians had their own ideas of right and wrong and justice, just as they had their own attitude toward outside prosecutors and judges, and nothing whatever could have induced them to testify against Natalio.

On the witness stand, the people who had been in the hut declared without wavering that they had not seen the person who threw the bomb. When they were asked by the desperate prosecutor whether they thought Natalio might have done it, they said the bomb might have been thrown by a former lover of the Crespo woman, a man known throughout the state for his jealous nature and hot temper. He was, they said, a man who was ready to do anything if he felt insulted.

Filomena went further still. She said she had known Natalio very well, since she had been his esposa for a couple of years, and that she was absolutely sure he would never do such a thing, that he would, in fact, be the last man on earth to do so. She said she was certain Natalio had never had an affair with the Crespo woman, that she could not even imagine he might have wanted to do the Crespo woman any harm. Natalio, she said solemnly, was not of a violent nature, but was, instead, surely the most peaceful man she could think of.

The prosecutor stared at Filomena unbelievingly. "The prosecution rests," he said.

Natalio's attorney, provided by the state, had not said one word so far. Now he rose and said, "The defense rests also!"

The jury retired. Less than an hour later, because they had business to attend to, they returned.

"Not guilty!" the foreman said.

Natalio was set free immediately. Then he and the witnesses, including Filomena and her new man, went to the nearest bar to celebrate the acquittal with two bottles of mezcal. The bottles passed from mouth to mouth, no one bothering with a glass, though now and then one of them would put a pinch of salt between his teeth.

After the bottles were empty, Natalio returned to his job. There was still a few hours of his working day left, and he, honest miner that he was, did not want to miss them.

On the first Saturday night following the trial, Natalio attended a dance in the village. There he found a pretty young woman who pleased him greatly. After Natalio had danced with her twice, he asked her to live with him as his wife.

The next day she arrived at his hut bringing with her all her belongings in a sugar sack, which she hung up on a peg. Once settled, she looked around the hut, cleaned the floor, and began to prepare supper.

While the beans were cooking, Natalio lay down, and stared up at the ceiling.

Supper ready, the woman put the steaming beans on the table.

Suddenly, as she turned back toward the hearth, she saw lying in the middle of the earthen floor a large tin can to which a smoking fuse was attached.

The woman escaped unhurt. Of Natalio Salvatorres, though, not even so much as a shirt button was ever found for the woman to remember him by.

The Diplomat *

During the rule of the dictator Porfirio Diaz, Mexico had neither bandits nor rebels nor train robbers. Porfirio Diaz had
rid the country of bandits in a very simple and effective dictatorial way. He had forbidden all newspapers to print a word
about bandit attacks, unless the report was sent to them by
the government itself.

Occasionally Porfirio Diaz was interested that reports
should appear about bandit attacks and train robberies. He
wanted, on those occasions, to provide booty for some general
whom he needed for particular political purposes connected
with keeping himself in power. He would then send such a
general and his troops into the bandit-troubled region. This
provided such a favored general with a small additional income of several times ten thousand dollars.

When the general had finished his business and had the
money in his pocket—collected from all the business people
of the region, who had to pay for the anti-bandit action at the
rates billed to them by the general—then all over the world

*Translated from the German
by Mina C. & H. Arthur Klein

appeared news reports that the great statesman Porfirio Diaz once again with iron hand had cleansed the land of bandits. Thus foreign capital was as safe in Mexico as if it lay in the vaults of the Bank of England.

Several dozen bandits had been shot—among them many who weren't bandits at all, but only agricultural laborers who had begun to rise to throw off the cruel yoke of the big landowners, the possessors of the great *latifundia*. About fifty names of other bandits who had been executed were published in the newspapers to facilitate the general's collection of the bills he had rendered. These names seemed authentic. They suffered only from the drawback that they lacked live bearers, for the general's secretary had either copied them from old tombstones, or simply thought them up.

At that time, more than today, paymasters, managers, and engineers of big American companies in Mexico were kidnapped and carried off into the mountains, with threats that they'd be chopped into bits if their ransom wasn't delivered on the spot within six days. It was Porfirio Diaz who paid the ransom to the bandits, so that American newspapers would not learn about the kidnappings and thus frighten off foreign capital. The ransomed man, once set free, was given a small sum in cash as compensation for his pains and as hush money.

But Porfirio Diaz did not dig down into his own pocket for these ransom and hush-money payments. If he had done that, he'd not have been able to gain the reputation of administering the national treasury with exceptional economy. Consequently he collected sums equal to the expended ransom and hush money from the same American companies for whose benefit—or rather for the benefit of their kidnapped employees—he had laid it out. To these companies he sold, for large amounts of good money, special concessions and communal land that he took from the Indians.

In this way he gained two new friends who were interested in the perpetuation of his dictatorship. One new friend was the favored American company; the other new friend was the Mexican large landowner, who, because the communal land had been taken from the Indians, gained a new troop of slaves whom he worked for three centavos a day, de Sol a Sol—from sunrise to sunset.

What newspapers do not report, simply does not exist. Especially not for foreign countries. Thus a nation always retains its good name. All dictators operate according to the same recipe. Today, as then, all the newspapers of Mexico, without exception, are in the hands of conservatives, in the hands of members of that class which praises the dictatorship of Porfirio Diaz as "Mexico's golden age." And because in Mexico this class is beginning to totter before the onslaught of the Indian and half-Indian proletariat, so today the newspapers of this class are filled with stories about bandits, rebels, and attacks on railway trains. They glorify every shabby assassin and every dishonorable general, if he happens to be a person who makes trouble for the present government.

Today in Mexico—according to the statements of those newspapers—complete freedom of the press is constantly endangered. Under the dictatorship of Porfirio Diaz, on the other hand, in spite of the rigid bans against reports about bandits, there was no talk about threats to the freedom of the press. For in those days there existed the only true and genuine freedom of the press—that glorified freedom of the press which operates in the interests of the capitalist class and permits the press to be free only to serve that interest.

In spite of the fact that Porfirio Diaz had completely exterminated all bandits in his simple and effective fashion, things nevertheless took place from time to time which had extremely painful consequences and which threatened to cause the collapse of his beautiful gold-plated construction—a construction lovelier and more skillful than a Prince Potemkin ever managed to create.

A new trade treaty was about to be negotiated between Mexico and the United States. With regard to all such treaties, Porfirio Diaz believed that he was the sly fox and consummate statesman; but when they were concluded and one looked more closely at a treaty and all its consequences, it was always found that Mexico had been tricked and robbed.

The United States government sent to Mexico one of its best commercial diplomats, for in the commercial relationships of the United States, Mexico is always regarded as one of the most important countries. For all time—in the future far more than in the past—Mexico will remain the most important country for the United States. More important than all of Europe.

Porfirio Diaz wanted to do a good lather job on this diplomat from the United States in order—as he thought—to give him a closer shave later on. And at the same time, Diaz wanted to display for that diplomat the wealth of Mexico and of its population—or of its upper classes, constituting less than one half of one percent of its population—and to demonstrate also how cultivated and civilized they were. Therefore, Diaz arranged a luxurious banquet in honor of the commercial diplomat from the United States.

Probably few men understood so well as Diaz how to mount such affairs. The later celebration which he staged in 1910 for all the world—the so-called Centenario celebration, the centenary of the independence of Mexico from Spain—unquestionably belongs among the greatest public celebrations which until then had been staged on the American continent, if not on the entire earth. Everything so abounded in and gleamed with gold that the visitors from other countries were dazzled.

The millions of dollars which that celebration cost the people of Mexico have never been counted. The visitors saw only the rich gold façades. In exceptionally clever ways, precautions were taken so that no foreign visitor to the Centenary had an opportunity to see what really lay behind the golden façades. Behind those façades ninety-five percent of the Mexican people lived in rags and tatters; ninety-five percent of the people had no shoes or boots; ninety-five percent lived only on tortillas, frijoles, chili, pulque, and tea made from the leaves of trees; more than eighty-five percent could not read; and more than eighty-five percent could not even write their own names.

Where in all the world, civilized or uncivilized, has ever

such an event been celebrated! And what a tiny, obscure village fiddler Prince Potemkin was, compared with this great blower of fanfares, Porfirio Diaz, who on the occasion of that centenary celebration of Mexican independence had his chest so loaded with medals and decorations from all the kings and kaisers that sixty fully loaded railway freight cars would not suffice to transport those orders and symbols of honor. Such is the picture of a golden age.

You have to admit that Porfirio Diaz understood how to hold festivals, and the event which he gave a few years earlier for that diplomat from the United States was an appropriate preliminary celebration to the glorious façade-illumination of the centenary festival.

The affair in honor of the diplomat was held in the Chapultepec Palace of Mexico City. Since the Revolution that palace has been rather neglected. Celebrations are now rarely held there, because the Mexican people today have more important things to do than to celebrate glittering affairs of this kind. For the most part, the Palace of Chapultepec is only a museum for foreign tourists who want to view the bed of the Empress Carlota, wife of Maximilian, and want to feel it to find out whether Carlota's sleeping accommodations were sufficiently soft.

Here also was the summer residence of the Aztec emperor, whose bath is still to be seen and is well preserved. Although Chapultepec Palace is the official residence of the President of the Republic of Mexico, the revolutionary presidents seldom live there. President Calles, for example, never lived in that palace, but occupied a modest house nearby.

Under Porfirio Diaz, however, things went on merrily and splendidly in Chapultepec Palace. Diaz was obliged to keep the small but very fat aristocracy of his country cozy and contented, in order to maintain his rule, just as other dictators have to warm up to the Pope when the capitalists, as a result of business going ever more badly, begin to realize that dictatorship too has its disadvantages.

To the affair given in honor of the diplomat from the

United States of America, only the cream of the top society of Mexico was invited, in order to intensify the diplomat's impression of how elegant, civilized, cultivated, and wealthy the Mexicans were. Glittering generals' uniforms abounded. And Porfirio Diaz himself, bedecked with gold braid and gold lace, looked like a circus ape playing the principal role in a burlesque operetta, set in some fabulous and fictitious Balkan principality.

The ladies were loaded with jewels like the main display case in the show window of a jeweler in one of the most elegant streets of Paris between two and six of an afternoon. All in all, those present were the most select society that Porfirio Diaz possibly could assemble.

It was not the first time in the life of the United States diplomat that he had been assigned to negotiate and complete trade treaties with other countries. Only a short time before he had successfully completed a trade treaty between his own nation and England. In this treaty, without the diplomat or the American government understanding quite how, England had captured the juiciest morsels, which England always succeeds in getting in all such, or similar, instances.

And in order to reward the United States diplomat for his good work and to honor him and hypnotize him until the trade treaty was signed and ratified by the legislative bodies of both countries, he was received in a private audience by the King of England. Since the King could not elevate him to a knighthood—a good republican American doesn't stand for that sort of thing—the King bestowed on him a gold pocket watch richly set with diamonds and provided with a resounding and distinguished dedication and with the engraved signature of Edward VII, King of England and Emperor of India.

The diplomat was naturally very proud of this watch, just as every good North American republican is proud when a European king or grand duke has showed him some attention. For after all, such news is carried on the front pages of all American newspapers.

It was quite natural that at the Chapultepec affair in his

honor, the diplomat showed this watch to Don Porfirio Diaz. Don Porfirio was flattered that the United States government considered him important enough to send to Mexico a diplomat of such distinction as to have been signally honored by the King of England, in order to negotiate and complete a new commercial treaty with him. Thereby Porfirio Diaz felt himself highly honored, since he was being regarded as of equal importance with the King of England.

Such equal status with kings and emperors made Porfirio Diaz tractable—a fact which was well known to the governments of all foreign countries and to their diplomats, and which fact was ruthlessly exploited by all governments and diplomats to the great detriment of the people of Mexico. Because Porfirio Diaz, like the majority of all dictators, was a parvenu upstart who had no well-founded right to be included among the aristocracy of Mexico—neither by virtue of his origin, nor his family, nor his education and training, nor his wealth, nor his talents. The characteristic which he did have in greatest abundance, however, was vanity.

As Diaz looked at the diplomat's watch, he was already reflecting how he, Diaz, could surpass this gift from the King of England, and in what form so that all nations on earth could hear of it and spread the word.

All the assembled Mexican generals naturally examined the watch and admired it appropriately.

After the preliminary ceremonies of greeting and presentation were over, the company withdrew to the great banquet where many fine speeches were made about the admirable relations between Mexico and the United States and between Mexico and all the other nations. Every participating diplomat, in his formal address, praised the golden age of Mexico, and above all the man who was solely responsible for the golden age—and that, of course, was none other than Don Porfirio himself.

When this was over, all prepared for the great ball which was danced in a style modeled after receptions for ambassadors in Paris. For Don Porfirio despised everything Mexican or Indian, and was an admirer of all that had a French aroma or which resembled court life in Vienna. This admiration at times reached total idiocy. Proof: The opera house of Mexico City.

During a pause in the great ball, the United States diplomat suddenly noticed that his valuable presentation watch was not where it originally had been. In spite of long agitated searching, he found it in none of the other pockets of his dress suit. And when he looked more closely later on, he found that the watch had been very expertly severed from the gold chain to which it had been secured—and indeed, as detectives later established, with the help of a manicure scissors.

The United States diplomat had sufficient tact to know that you didn't mention such a thing if it concerns only a run-of-the-mill gold watch that is lost during so lofty a diplomatic social event. You give a little wink, perhaps, to tip off the master of ceremonies. If the watch is recovered, all well and good; if it is not found, then the loss is made good by the U. S. State Department. Such incidents occur more often than the average citizen, who has never been a guest at a diplomatic ball, would believe, for diplomats too—more than one would think—are frequently in financial difficulties, which can be taken care of only in ways that do not conform completely to the proprieties expected at ambassadors' balls.

This watch, however, could not be replaced. That a diplomat treasures so little the personal gift of the King of England as to lose it, is almost an insult to the King of England. It could result in the loss of his diplomatic good name and diplomatic position. Now, from a United States diplomat one cannot expect the tact of a French, English, or Russian diplomat. The French diplomat would find a witty excuse to explain how and in what way the watch was mislaid, an excuse so fine and elegant that it would be more likely to help than to hinder him in his diplomatic career.

But in this area we from the United States are still peasants and schoolboys, and consequently make a fuss about it.

With the blunt toughness in matters of tact that is characteristic of the people of his country, the United States diplomat turned at once to Don Porfirio, and, with the help of his

Spanish-speaking secretary, asked him for a brief conference.

"Pardon me, Don Porfirio," the diplomat said. "I am truly sorry that I must bother you, but I have just been robbed, here in this room, of my watch that was presented to me by the King of England."

Porfirio Diaz did not move a muscle. He refrained from saying "That's impossible!" or "Isn't there some mistake?" He knew his people and no one was more aware than he that only in the newspaper reports had bandits been eliminated, but not, however, in the land of Mexico. For if he had wanted to exterminate all the bandits, he would have had to begin by shooting all his own generals and governors and mayors and tax administrators and secretaries of state. The ruling class robbed because of insatiable greed; and the non-ruling class robbed of bitter hunger.

Hence Porfirio Diaz said in answer to the diplomat only, "Don't worry, your Excellency. This is clearly just a little joke. I give you my word of honor that within forty-eight hours you shall have the watch in your possession once again."

The word of honor of the President! Porfirio Diaz could confidently give his word of honor. Whoever is master of all bandits and thieves, whoever knows all bandits and thieves and their tricks and dodges as well as did Porfirio Diaz—himself a master-thief in all matters not directly involving common pickpocketry—would surely be able to find the watch.

Finally, and with the politest possible manner, Porfirio Diaz said farewell to the diplomat from North America, without having mentioned, even by a tiny word, the little misfortune.

However, afterwards, though only his most intimate aides were aware of it, Don Porfirio began to rage, as only he could rage. It was the raging of a dictator whose frauds are on the verge of being exposed.

"The Old Boy is blowing his top again," the frightened servants whispered to each other, and they trembled in fear at what would happen when the ball was over. The dictator's outbursts of rage were dreaded more than earthquakes, since he became as vicious as an angry old wildcat.

What he knew from the start, and with complete certainty, was this: a Mexican had the watch; only a Mexican could have it. And, to be sure, he knew how to handle Mexican thieves.

If the watch had been taken by a member of the staff of servants in his palace, then it was already too late to order the many detectives not to allow any of the servants to leave the palace. If the watch actually had been stolen by a servant, the detectives were no longer of any use, for, in the meantime, the watch already would have been smuggled out of the palace. Admittedly, it was also possible that one of the detectives had the watch. It was by no means certain that detectives would not steal what they could get hold of easily. Porfirio Diaz, after all, had placed plenty of thieves, pickpockets, burglars, and highwaymen in the ranks of the police, because thieves often make better thief-catchers than do respectable people.

It was hardly likely that the diamonds would be pried out of the watch or that its case would be broken up so that the watch could be sold more easily and safely piece by piece. The value of the watch would be diminished too much. It was more likely that the engraved inscription would be eradicated before the watch reappeared and was offered for sale. Stripped of its engraved inscription, however, the watch would naturally be worthless to the diplomat.

Don Porfirio could have immediately got hold of another gold watch, studded with any required number of diamonds, if only that would have served the diplomat's needs. But as things were, it was necessary to recover this particular watch, and no other.

Porfirio Diaz gave way to rage not because he feared he might perhaps be unable to recover the watch. Getting it back he regarded as a problem that he could solve. No, what caused him to boil with rage was something else. The theft of the watch at such a time and place stripped off the gilt veneer from one of his gleaming façades. It exposed nakedly the ordinary and unmistakable cheap plaster beneath.

The whole world had been overawed by the legend that Porfirio Diaz, the great Mexican statesman, with iron hand and broom of steel had completely and permanently purged

the country of bandits and thieves with such success as had
never been attained by any other person in any other country.

According to the news reports that Porfirio Diaz had
spread throughout the world, at that time in Mexico one
could travel on a horse with a sack full of gold pieces on the
right side and another on the left side, from one end of the
Republic to the other, and when one arrived one would
have additional sacks of gold pieces on the right side as
well as on the left—one sack more on each side than one
had on the day of one's departure.

In a certain sense this was true. A capitalist from the
United States, who crossed from El Paso, Texas, into Mexico
with fifty thousand dollars in checks, could leave Mexico via
Nogales six weeks later with one hundred thousand dollars in
checks—the surplus having been squeezed out of Mexico and
its people in that short time with the help of Porfiro Diaz.

But strictly and literally speaking, under Porfirio Diaz it
was unsafe to travel through Mexico with money or other
valuables, without a military escort. Often enough, the military escort when still under way would begin to reflect that it
was wiser to protect itself with the money than to protect the
money. Then a report would appear—if the matter could not
be taken care of privately by the Diaz government to the sat-
isfaction of all concerned—that the stagecoach had bogged
down in a swamp or been buried by a landslide.

However, the whole lovely web of lies in which the dictatorship had enveloped itself, was threatening to come apart,
since at a diplomatic social event within Chapultepec Palace
itself, a gold watch had been stolen from the pocket of so important a diplomat from the United States of America—for
this meant that the property of an honored foreign diplomat
was not safe even at a diplomatic party in Mexico.

If bandits were so close to the throne of the dictator himself, what must things be like elsewhere in the land of Mexico? If this incident should be reported in the American newspapers, then the whole world would learn that the iron hand
of Porfirio Diaz was really only made of cardboard, and that

the big foreign capitalists would be wiser to be cautious with investments, so far as Mexico was concerned.

The diplomat from the United States had the dictator's word of honor and his statement that this amounted only to a little joke. Therefore the diplomat said not a word about it to reporters because he felt that it was his duty to wait to find whether, and in what manner, Porfirio Diaz would make good his word of honor. Porfirio Diaz knew that, according to the custom in diplomatic circles, the American was bound to leak nothing to the Mexican press, as long as the matter was covered by the dictator's word of honor.

That same night, Porfirio Diaz summoned the police chief to discuss with him how the watch could be recovered without advertising in the newspapers.

The next morning began the plowing up of the Mexican land in the search for the American diplomat's stolen watch.

The police chief appeared in Belén. Belén is the largest prison in Mexico City where all male and female criminals are held until sentenced.

The police chief had all prisoners assembled, and he addressed them as follows:

"Yesterday evening a gold watch was stolen. The watch is inlaid with diamonds. On the inside of the cover a dedication is engraved in English. This dedication includes the signature of King Edward VII.

"It is now seven o'clock in the morning. If, by seven o'clock this evening the watch is turned over to the warden of this prison, then you'll all be released tonight—and none of you will be prosecuted for the crime for which you now find yourself in Belén.

"The one who returns the watch won't be asked for his name. He'll be allowed to leave as freely as he came. He won't be asked how he got hold of the watch, and he won't be either prosecuted or imprisoned because of the watch nor for anything else he may have committed before seven o'clock this morning. Besides, he'll receive from the warden a reward of two hundred pesos in gold.

"You will now all receive writing paper and an envelope and pencils. You may write in these letters anything you want. The letters will not be read or censored. And nobody on the prison staff will be allowed to read even the address on the envelope. In an hour, the letter carriers will be here, and you personally will turn over to them the letters you have written. The letters will be handled as official state secrets and delivered as addressed.

"Here I have a certificate, signed by Don Porfirio, by me, and by the warden of this prison. This certificate has the force of law until seven-thirty this evening."

The speech by the chief of police and the certificate, which contained it all word for word, proved how intimately Don Porfirio knew his thieves and bandits. If the watch really were in the hands of common pickpockets and fences for stolen goods, then it would be delivered by seven that evening, or even earlier.

In Mexico, as in other countries, all thieves and fences are quite well acquainted with one another. If one alone does not know all the others, still he knows at least about twenty others, knows their hideouts, their hangouts, their taverns, and where they live—knows where those twenty can be found, knows their sweethearts, and knows what each one of them has to answer for. Each of these twenty, in turn, knows a number of others with whom the first one is not acquainted.

For these reasons—and here neither Don Porfirio nor the police chief was mistaken—it was certain the contents of that speech became known within only a few hours to all thieves in Mexico City as well as to all fences for stolen goods.

The letters written by the prisoners to their accomplices on the outside—and delivered without censorship or inspection—contained everything that the prisoners had long wanted to tell their accomplices living in freedom outside.

To the great distress of the prisoners, and probably to the even greater distress of Porfirio Diaz, the watch was not delivered by the stipulated time. In this instance, failure resulted from the methods that Porfirio Diaz previously had used with success in cases that seemed hopeless.

The story was later told in Mexico that the watch really was recovered in this way with the help of the prisoners, and that all the prisoners were freed as they had been promised. But this is not correct. This rumor was only spread in order to hide the truth.

When by seven o'clock that evening the stolen watch had not been returned, Porfirio Diaz knew for certain that the watch had not been stolen by common thieves and also that it was not in the hands of the fences. He concluded, and quite rightly, that the watch was in the hands of someone who needed money, but did not need it so urgently that he had to hurry to sell the watch. It was someone who knew enough to correctly assess the value of the watch, and who awaited the time when he could sell it as advantageously as possible for a second-hand timepiece.

With the common or small-time thieves now ruled out, Porfirio Diaz knew the next level of thieves who had to be considered. These were not the last resorts, but rather that group who approach most closely to the common thieves and highwaymen, in terms of morality and incessant need for money, as well as with regard to impudence in stealing whenever an opportunity presented itself.

Accordingly, Don Porfirio now summoned to an evening audience all the generals who had been present at the diplomatic party to enliven it with their gold-laden uniforms. He had a list of those generals who had been in the Palace and he saw to it that all of them attended this audience.

But as matters turned out, one was missing—a Divisional general, or Divisionario. This Divisionario sent his regrets. Don Porfirio accepted those regrets because they arose from pressing duties that could not be postponed.

To the assembled generals Don Porfirio spoke: "Caballeros, probably all of you saw here in the palace the watch that the American diplomat showed me. This watch was lost track of in the palace. I assume that one of the soldiers on guard duty or one of your orderlies found the watch. That watch must be in my hands tomorrow morning by ten o'clock. If it is in my hands by that indicated time, then, caballeros, each of you will receive a special bonus of one thousand dollars for your efforts. Also I will seek to show my appreciation to you in other ways.

"Naturally, you will take care of this matter as unobtrusively as lies within your powers; for I do not want even the tiniest stain to fall upon our glorious army. With the offenders, you will proceed according to your own judgment. I thank you, caballeros!"

Everyone who knows Mexico knows that some Mexican soldiers of the lower ranks may have every possible vice and depravity; that—especially in matters connected with their love-life—they will unhesitatingly murder a rival. Mexican soldiers steal. That is true. But they steal only that which—and not more than—their generals and other superior officers leave over for them to steal.

In their ethics, in their bravery, in their honor, in their love of their homeland, in their loyalty, they stand far higher than their generals. They are used by the false and dishonorable generals to attack and to murder their own brothers, fathers, sons, mothers, comrades in other regiments. They never know whether in fact they are on the side of rebelling generals or on the side of troops that have remained loyal. They fight, because they remain loyal to their general, because they bear within themselves a fidelity their generals do not have.

Their generals initiate a military revolt under the slogan of freeing the tormented country from tyrants and from the "Bolshies"; whereas in actual practice they perpetrate revolts only in order to plunder the banks and the prosperous business people, and they have conveyed the stolen property safely to the United States, before the troops that have remained loyal to the government can pursue and catch up with them within the remote districts of the large land of Mexico. Under generals of this sort, the Mexican soldier—who can be regarded as the bravest, most loyal, and least demanding soldier of all armies on earth—is forced to serve and to obey.

Porfirio Diaz knew well, as the assembled generals also knew, that the slandered common soldiers might have all manner of vices and depravities, but one thing they certainly were not—pickpockets.

And consequently Porfirio Diaz knew quite well that when he beat the sack, he meant the donkey. In other words, when he implicated the rank-and-file soldiers he meant the generals.

In every lost war, the rank-and-file soldiers are always blamed for the defeat. It is always the rank-and-file soldiers, the proletarians, who would not stand their ground, whose morale was shattered, who lent a willing ear to defeatist misleaders and apostles of peace, who had no love for the fatherland. Never is the blame laid on the incompetent generals, never on the politicians with hardened arteries, never on the weak-spined and demoralized diplomats, never on the greedy profiteers. Always the fault is that of the soldier, the proletarian. And if the war is won, then that is wholly and solely thanks to the competent generals, the wise statesmen, and clever diplomats. The generals, statemen, and diplomats get all the honors recorded in world history and school textbooks. The ordinary soldier gets as reward a parade, which the half-starved, lousy, and crippled munitions workers are allowed to witness like obedient sheep, behind a heavily barricaded line of police who swing their clubs in order that the generals are supplied with enough "Hurrah!" shouters and wavers of red, white, and blue star-spangled flags.

The generals here knew right well that Porfirio Diaz did not for an instant mean seriously that one of the soldiers on guard or one of the generals' orderlies could have stolen the watch. Admittedly, all the generals knew what Porfirio Diaz really thought of them, just as Porfirio Diaz most certainly knew what all his generals thought of him. Master and accomplices both bore down heavily with feet, fists, and claws on the unfortunate rich land of Mexico.

By ten o'clock next morning the watch had not been returned.

For an instant—but only for an instant—Porfirio Diaz became confused, because it seemed that he had miscalculated.

Then, however, he recalled the Divisional general who had sent his regrets at being unable to be on hand the evening before, because he had to be out of the capital, in Tlalpam, on an important matter connected with the military service.

Now Porfirio Diaz speedily ordered this general to appear.

When the general stood before him, Porfirio Diaz looked at him for a while, then said, short and hard, "Divisionario, give me the watch that belongs to the American diplomat."

Without a change of expression, without in any way becoming embarrassed, the general reached under the jacket of his uniform, poked around in a pocket there, and brought out the watch.

He stepped two paces closer to the dictator and handed him the watch with the words, "A sus apreciables órdenes, Señor Presidente, at your highly valued service."

Porfirio Diaz took the watch and laid it on the table in front of him.

He felt called upon to say something. And so he said: "Divisionario, I don't understand—eh—why?"

The Divisionario thereupon answered soberly, "I was afraid Señor Presidente, that someone else would take the watch, and so I thought to myself, it may be better if I take it.

To this answer Porfirio Diaz remained silent. In so doing, he proved again most admirably that he was smarter than many of those who condemn him wish to admit. Also it is difficult to assume that Porfirio Diaz would have been involved in a matter of common pocket-picking. And certainly not in the final five years of his rule, when he had already become a little shaky.

But one thing must be said.

Porfirio Diaz had to keep the diplomat in a friendly mood and in a favorable frame of mind if the incident was not to become known. Porfirio Diaz was more concerned about the good name of his court than many a European potentate. Therefore, in order to appease the diplomat and put him in a good humor, Porfirio was obliged, when it came to the completion of the commercial treaty, to make concessions for which, it is true, the people of Mexico had to pay, but which brought to that diplomat the honor of being called one of the most skillful diplomats of the United States of America.

Frustration

Mercedes, wearing her wedding dress, stood before the mirror, which was not large enough to reflect her whole figure all at the same time. The wedding dress, bought at a bargain sale, was pretty, and in good taste. She had every reason to feel proud in it.

She was twenty-two, Mexican-born, but had lived in this Texas town since being brought here as a baby. She had worked as a chambermaid at the same hotel for the last six years, but had decided not to give up her job after her forthcoming marriage.

"Play it safe," one of her more experienced fellow workers had warned her. "You don't know how the guy is going to turn out, Meche. Before you even realize, you may have to come crawling on your knees to get your old job back. Ask me. I sure oughta know. I've been hitched three times and it never clicked."

Mercedes had met Anselmo, American-born, but of Mexican parents, at a festival of the Mexican colony on the eve of their own Independence Day. It was a very gay and

crowded party, perfect in every way. They had been introduced to one another by mutual acquaintances.

Out of this meeting had grown a serious love between
the two, culminating four months later in their engagement to
be married.

Anselmo worked as chauffeur to a rich family residing
on "The Hill," in the elegant west side of the city.

The date for the wedding had been set three weeks before, and the ceremony was to take place this very day at St.
Mary's, the church preferred by most of the Mexicans living
in this town.

Today was the day which Mercedes expected for the rest
of her life to look back to as the greatest and happiest of her
existence on earth.

A girl friend of hers, also Mexican, but living in another
section of the city, had come to help her dress.

"I can't stay long, you know, Meche. Got to be at the
café at twelve. The boss is an awful mug. He'll start yelling
even if I'm only two minutes late."

"That's all right, Esther. I'm almost ready. Anselmo
will be here any minute now. The wedding is to be at
eleven sharp."

"Yes, I know. And look at the time—ten minutes to
eleven, and he's not here yet. What's wrong with this guy?"

Mercedes sighed. "Late as usual. He'll never be a real
American. He promised to be here by half past ten. He took
three days off: today, tomorrow, and the day after tomorrow.
That's what he told me Saturday night when I saw him last,
and we talked over the details."

"Maybe he and the two witnesses stepped into a joint for
a drink to get up his courage."

"What should he need courage for? He loves me. And he
knows perfectly well that I love him even more."

"Well, honey, it's striking eleven now. Perhaps he's giving you the slip at the last minute. Looks that way to me."

"He? Anselmo? The gate? Me? Never. Never in his
whole life. He knows that I couldn't live without him and that
I'd die if he walked out on me."

"Boloney! He wouldn't be the first and won't be the last.

Those rascals. None of them is worth dying for. What's your watch say? Mine is a quarter past eleven."

"Same here." Mercedes looked up from her wristwatch, stared at Esther, and bit her lip.

"I'll lay you three to one that your chauffeur is stinking drunk, if you ask me." Esther grabbed her little handbag. "Well, Meche, I'm afraid I've got to beat it now. Got to hurry home first before showing up at work. Damn it, how I hate rattling dishes and throwing big smiles at sour-looking quick lunchers. Well, honey, you know, I don't have to tell you: all the best of luck to you, the very best. May the most Holy Virgin bless you, dear."

They threw their arms around each other and kissed.

"Don't you worry, Meche, everything will be okay. Byebye, got to hurry. Good luck again!"

Mercedes was left alone in her little two-room-and-kitchen apartment.

Half past eleven now.

She decided to find a taxi to take her to the church and see whether Anselmo might be waiting for her there. As she ran toward the door, her feet became entangled in her long wedding dress.

"I can't very well go alone to the church with this dress on. If Anselmo isn't there waiting for me, I'd die of shame," she muttered, hurrying to change as though the wedding dress were on fire.

Out on the street she hailed a taxi. Arriving at the church, she entered and looked around. All she saw was a few women worshipers kneeling before images.

She ran to the vestry and spoke to Father Justino who was to marry them.

"No, daughter. He hasn't been here, nor in the church as far as I know. Yes, of course, I know the young man to whom you refer. Perhaps he met with an accident or was delayed otherwise. His employer may have had urgent need of his services, my child . . . don't you worry . . . everything will turn out all right. Of course, daughter, of course; any time you say. I'll be at your assistance any time day or night. I live right next door, yes, in that little house. Just come, you two, knock at the door any time, and I'll marry you. Go with God, my daughter."

"Thank you, padre." Mercedes kissed his hand and hurried back home.

Anselmo was not there. Nor had he been there while she was looking for him in the church.

Fear overcame her. Something must have happened to him. Something terrible. Even Father Justino had hinted at the possibility of an accident.

From a drugstore phone booth she called the home of Anselmo's boss.

"No, miss," answered a man's voice, "he hasn't been in all night . . . no, he wasn't here this morning either. You know, he got three days off, until day after tomorrow. No, miss, I don't know why. He said he had some important personal business to attend to. . . . What did you say, miss? . . . Did I get you right? . . . He was going to be married? To you, miss? . . . Don't you think there must be a slight mistake, miss, sorry to say so? . . . It's news to me. We ought to know, miss. . . . He's been going with one of our lady's maids. Long? Oh yes, for quite some time. We understand they're going to get married soon. Yes, they're engaged to be married, if I may say so. All the servants know about it. And as a matter of fact I understand they went on a picnic today. Yes, miss, just the two of them, all alone by themselves. No, miss, this is the butler speaking. Sorry, miss, I'll have to hang up. The lady is calling me. Not at all, miss . . . don't mention it. What did you say your name was? Of course, if you don't wish me to tell him. Of course, I shall refrain from doing so. You're welcome, quite welcome, miss, I'm sure. Good-bye."

Mercedes felt as though she were going to pass out in the stuffy little phone booth. She leaned against the wall, weak and empty.

A pounding on the door of the booth brought her to her senses. "Hey, sister, if you want to sleep there, please step up to the desk and register. I'll see that you get a cot brought in."

Opening the door, she said: "I'll be all right, excuse me, mister."

The druggist, seeing her deadly white face, immediately changed his tone. "I didn't know, miss, excuse me, please. Can I do something for you? I'll mix you something to straighten you out. Just say so, miss. I'm sorry. Awfully sorry. Anything you wish, miss."

"Much obliged. I'm all right. Quite all right. Sure. Thank you."

Home again, she threw herself on the bed. She thought of killing herself, of killing Anselmo, of killing the lady's maid, of killing his boss, of butchering the butler, of setting fire to the hotel she worked for.

Finally, she fell into a deep sleep.

She slept for two days without once waking.

Since, because of the wedding, she had taken her annual vacation, nobody came to see her, everyone assuming that she was away on her honeymoon trip.

When, on the morning of the third day, she finally got out of bed, she felt fully refreshed and as young and strong as ever. Only her head felt swollen as though there were something inside it that didn't belong there. It didn't disturb her, though, not in the least, even though she had never felt this way before. With the help of a couple of aspirins the numbness in her head would be sure to disappear. Also, a stiff drink in the evening would do her lots of good.

Sitting on the bed and gazing vaguely around her, her eyes became fixed on the open closet and the wedding dress which she had hastily and carelessly hung there.

She took it off the hook, laid it across the table, and straightened it out. Not satisfied with the results, she ironed it neatly. While doing so, she began, softly at first, to hum a tune. Soon she changed to another, until, after a few minutes, she was singing gaily at the top of her voice, changing from one song to another as they came to mind.

Presently she stepped in front of the mirror, smiled at herself, arranged her abundant hair as attractively as she could, and made up her face with utmost care. All the while, she hummed and sang unceasingly, a very happy, contented woman.

Next she packed the dress and all she needed to go with

it, into a suitcase and, taking a taxi, hurried to a photographer whom she had selected from an advertisement weeks before to take her wedding picture.

"I want you to take my picture in my wedding dress."

"Glad to, miss—or," with a broad grin, "or Mrs. already?"

"Mrs., please. I was married three days ago. I had no time for the picture then."

"I understand, madam." Again the photographer grinned. "I understand perfectly. Hurried off on a wedding trip? Am I right, madam, or am I?"

"That's it, sir. How did you know?"

"Experience, madam. Experience with a few hundred newlyweds." Stepping back two paces, he spread his arms, raised his eyes, and declaimed: "Oh, marriage, oh you sweet marriage, nothing on this wretched earth equals you, oh sweet marriage, making lovers overflow with eternal happiness." Then, as if emerging from a trance, he bowed, and said: "Pardon me, I'm so easily overcome by sentiment, seeing in my studio such a happy woman, madam. Excuse my emotion, I can't help it."

A few minutes after her picture was taken, the photographer showed her the proofs, which she found satisfactory.

"Of course, madam, they'll look much, much better when ready. Retouching, you know, Mrs. That's the real art, the way in which you can tell a high-class photographer. Will it be all right Monday, madam?"

"Suits me fine. How much did you say? Six dollars? There you are."

"Thanks, madam, thanks ever so much. I also have the reputation of being the best in town for taking baby pictures, madam, if the occasion should arrive. I'll be only too happy to give you excellent service in that line too."

"We'll talk about this in its own good time, sir."

"Of course, of course, madam. No offense meant, madam, excuse me. Understand, please, it's our business, you see, not only to get customers but also to hold them. You'll understand, madam, that I didn't mean to be indiscreet. Thank you, madam."

Mercedes hesitated. She was still in her wedding dress because the photographer had told her not to change until he was sure the picture had come out all right.

"I was thinking, sir," she said with hesitation.

"Yes, madam?"

"I was wondering whether you could also make another picture for me—I with my wedding dress on and my husband by my side. He can't come in right now because he's out of town driving his boss to Kansas City and will probably not return for several weeks. I have a picture of him with me."

The photographer looked at her mistrustfully.

"Of course, madam, I can make such a picture. It's called photomontage. It's rather unusual, though if I may say so. You're sure there's no catch to it somewhere?"

"I'm sorry, sir, I don't understand."

"You see, madam, such a picture might cause me lots of trouble. You must understand we've had cases, not I, no, never, but other fellows in our trade. I mean there have been cases in which such pictures as you want me to make have been used for criminal purposes—blackmail, all sorts of divorce scandals and other such things."

"Never mind, if you can't do it, I'll go somewhere else."

"I didn't say that, madam. I can easily make any kind of picture and be pleased to. If you would just assure me that there is no catch whatever, I mean no bad intention on your part. Why I'm all set to make the picture right away. . . . Where did you say you lived? . . . Oh yes, excuse me, I've jotted it down already. . . . And your husband, who did you tell me he slaves for?" He thought this to be a good occasion to grin once more.

"Well, as I was saying, madam, I'm sure there'll be no trouble, no trouble at all. Such pictures naturally are more expensive than direct pictures, because certain special processing is necessary. May I have a look at the picture of your husband."

She opened her suitcase and took out the picture, handing it to the photographer.

Glancing at it briefly, he said with a sigh of great relief: "No trouble at all, madam, I assure you. He's okay, your husband I mean. Good-looking fellow. Congratulations! Sorry, awfully sorry that I said something about bad intentions. I didn't mean to."

A week later Mercedes held the pictures in her hands. The one on which she appeared with her husband at her side had come out so naturally that only an expert, and perhaps not even he, would have seen anything phony in it.

Naturally, all her fellow workers at the hotel had to see the pictures.

"My! What do you think of that? There's a guy any girl could fall for," one of them exclaimed.

"You said it, dearie, that's why I grabbed him, and no fooling."

"Smart girl. Great, if it lasts."

"Don't you worry. It will. I'll attend to that. That's me!" Mercedes boasted, her fists pressed firmly on her hips.

Every day she had something new and interesting to tell the other girls about her husband: what he liked best for breakfast; what time he wanted his supper on his days off when he didn't eat at his employer's house; which movies he preferred; what were his favorite sports. She even told some of the girls with whom she had been working the longest, intimate details of her married life. These she told with such frankness and in such detail that Clara, oldest and most experienced of the girls, had to admit that she, Clara, was only a novice in comparison.

One year went by.

One morning, Mercedes entered the manager's office and asked for a six weeks' leave of absence.

"Why, what for?" he asked. "Going to Paris?" he added jokingly. "Have you acquired a wealthy friend?"

She blushed. "No, Mr. Leager. It's simply this way. How should I explain? Well. Can't you understand? I'm married more than a year now. We—I mean—I and my—we're going to have—we—you know, Mr. Leager, you're a married man yourself and you have children, haven't you?"

"Congratulations, Mercedes. Of course you may have

the six weeks off. Half pay goes with it. If you should need money, I can write you a check for fifty dollars."

"Thanks. I won't need it. I've saved up for the occasion. Thanks anyway."

"I hope it's a boy."

"I'd prefer a girl."

"Right. I, too, think a girl might be better, especially the first one. Well, when are you checking out? Bring in your substitute. Your place will be kept open for you. You know that. Don't you worry. You've been with us so long and we've never had any serious complaints. Well, congratulations again, and I hope everything goes well. Good luck."

"Well, Mercedes?" the manager asked, when, after six weeks, she reported for work again. "What is it, boy or girl?"

With a proud toss of her head, she said: "Boy, weighed eight and a half pounds when he arrived."

"Great woman. Happy? What? Don't tell me. All right, Mercedes, go back to your work. By the way—for the next four weeks you may run home once every three hours, provided you are back inside of thirty minutes each time."

"Oh, Mr. Leager, thanks. I can manage that fine by taking the bus. Thanks a lot for the consideration."

"Of course, that goes only for the next four weeks. After that, you'll have to arrange matters without interrupting your duties here."

"I understand. By that time everything will be settled anyhow, I'm sure. And once more, many thanks."

Whenever she received her wages now, the first thing she did was to buy a toy or little stockings or shoes or something of the sort. Before she bought these things, she would discuss them for days with her fellow workers. And the day after the purchase, she would tell how the boy had enjoyed it, how pretty he looked with the blue woolen cap on his head. She would talk at length about how quickly he was growing, how healthy he looked, on what occasion he had smiled for the first time, how the coming teeth were making him miserable.

As Mercedes kept up no intimate friendship with anybody except her fellow workers, and had no acquaintances to speak of, it happened very rarely that she had visitors at home. Esther, the girl who had been with her on the morning of her wedding day and whom she considered her only real friend, had left town shortly after that abortive wedding day to live with her older sister in Oklahoma City. Together they ran a lunch counter of their own there.

Mercedes was too reticent to make new friends easily. Her fellow workers were far too occupied with their own affairs to care for the details of how Mercedes lived. In any case, they saw enough of each other every day at work.

However, now and then, one of the girls, or a woman of the neighborhood, would drop by for a chat. None of these visitors ever stayed long. Mercedes had a way of cutting them short or putting them out that chilled any sort of intimate friendship, particularly if that friendship was sought within the walls of her home.

If, occasionally, one of the girls from the hotel stopped by, she would ask, naturally, to see the little boy. Mercedes would then say the boy was on the playground in the park where he had been sent with a woman of the neighborhood who had taken her kids there also and who would look after him. Another time she would say the boy was staying with his aunt, or with his grandmother, and that he was to remain there for a couple of weeks, perhaps to get a change of climate.

Yet the visitor would notice all the child's toys, and his clothes, some lying around, others well kept in the closet. And they would admire his pretty little bed, his own little table and chairs. It was the talk of all the hotel employees that there could hardly be a mother more devoted to her baby than Mercedes.

Occasionally there would be days when she would arrive in the morning all exhausted, asking the manager to let her off for the day or allow her to quit early because her baby had fever or a cold, or something else was wrong with him.

Next day, or two days later, she would report for work all radiant, for the boy had recovered and was well again.

The boy was now, according to Mercedes, six years old

and would be ready for school at the beginning of the next term.

"Gee, Meche, how time flies," one of the older chambermaids sighed, "one can hardly believe it. I still remember the day you were married. Now look. Your boy is going to school soon and before we'll even have time to shout 'what's biting me,' he'll go to college. Or won't you send him to college?"

"Won't I? What a silly question! What am I slaving for all these years if not to give the kid a real education. I want him to be an engineer or something like that, or one who builds huge houses. I only wonder if I can afford it. Matter of fact, lately I've been thinking of going into some sort of business of my own for the boy's sake, and to make more money. But I guess it'll be the hotel rooms until I kick off because of old age. No prospects here at this job. And what else could I do? I wonder. I'll try it anyhow one of these days."

"How long is it now that your husband died?"

"Six years. You remember he died shortly after the kid came."

"Yes, I do remember now, you've told us several times. Smashed up his car, or that of his boss. Wasn't that the way he finished up?"

"That's right," Mercedes confirmed with a deep sigh. "Please don't remind me. I haven't got over it yet."

Suddenly Mercedes fell sick. The doctor called it pneumonia, aggravated by tuberculosis in an advanced state.

She was taken to the hospital.

The doctors had no hope of saving her. The case developed such complications within twenty-four hours that the doctors thought they could predict the exact hour at which she would pass away.

Two days later she became delirious and developed very high fever. She tossed restlessly and began to scream for her little boy Rodolfo.

Her fellow workers, visiting her as frequently as their time would permit, brought her flowers and remained at her side for hours, trying to calm her in their own way, since the nurses had failed to have any quieting effect upon her. They also secured a private room for her, hoping to make her last two or three days of life as comfortable as possible.

On the first or second day of her delirium she had only occasionally screamed for her boy, now from the early hours of the third day on, she constantly howled and shouted to have him with her.

One of the girls tried to locate the boy, but failed. Now these chambermaids called for advice and help from the Sisters of St. Anne.

The Sisters of St. Anne were a body of Catholic women who gave help when ordinary charity and social welfare were unable to handle certain cases in which personal and spiritual problems were more important than monetary charity.

Two of these Sisters of St. Anne arrived at the hospital immediately. The doctor, accompanying them to the room where Mercedes lay slowly dying, said: "She has only about three more hours to live, with the help of two more injections, perhaps six hours, no longer. I leave the poor woman in your care, ladies. My mission is over. Sorry. Please do whatever you can to ease her end. The most humane thing you could do at this time would be to find her little boy and bring him here. Her friends, who can't stay away from their jobs too long, were unable to locate him. She is crying herself hoarse for him. She won't even recognize him. But she'll die a happy mother if she can just hold him in her arms for the last few minutes of her life. That's all, ladies. See what you can do."

One of the Sisters hurried to the address given her as that of the dying woman.

"Yes, miss, I'm her landlady all right. . . . No, miss, she doesn't owe me a cent. It's all paid, even two months in advance. She always has been my model tenant. . . . What boy are you talking about? Her boy? She had a boy? . . . Oh, yes, I know she has a little boy, six years or so he must be now. . . . You can see that for yourself. Her whole little apartment is full of the kid's things and clothes. . . . No, miss, sorry, I don't know where he is at present. I know for sure he's not in now. You see, miss, I don't actually live here permanently. I come here only to collect the rent. I live in another house of mine about ten blocks from here. . . . Not at all. You're welcome."

The Sister asked the neighbors. The boy was with none of them. Everybody in the neighborhood knew that Mercedes had a little boy about six years old about whom she always talked—but where he was to be found now, no one could say.

She ran back to the hospital and found Mercedes screaming for her boy more heartbreakingly than ever.

The doctor in charge arrived. "She wants to die. But she can't until she has held her boy once more in her arms. Then she will die immediately and quietly and suffer no more. And suffer she does terribly. She is burning up inside in a most horrible way. Do whatever you can. Bring a boy of his age. Any boy will do. She won't recognize him anyway. If she can only feel a boy in her arms she will fall asleep happily and never wake up again."

The Sister, remembering a family in her district with a boy of that age, hurried there and asked the mother's permission. Having obtained it, she dressed the boy in his best clothes and took him to the hospital.

Opening the door of Mercedes' room, she pushed the boy in, saying loudly: "Mercedes dear, here is your little boy, right here. Won't you speak to him?"

"Has he come at last? My baby, Rodolfo, my little boy, come here, come close to your mother. She is waiting for you. She has been waiting so long for you."

The boy started to cry and was ready to shout. "You're not my mother!" But the Sisters motioned him to be quiet, to just go near the bed and nothing would happen to him. "She is just a poor mother who has lost her boy and she doesn't know it."

Despite his age, the boy understood. He stepped closer, grasped Mercedes' hand and said: "Mommy! Mommy dear, here I am, beside your bed. Don't cry, Mommy. I've been playing outside, but now I'm here."

"Thank you, my baby, for coming at last. I've been waiting for you so very, very long. Now at last you're here and I can go to sleep. It's already late at night, and it's all dark. Don't cry, my baby. Mother will be all right tomorrow. Go and drink your milk. You'll find it as always standing on your little table. And don't gulp it. Drink slowly. I'm just a little tired now from so much work at the hotel. I'll sleep now. And you go to bed, too. And when you open your eyes in the morning I'll be with you and kiss you good morning as I always do, you know. Soon it will be Christmas. I'm tired, oh so very, very tired. Hold my hand for a while. Just for a little while until I'm asleep."

This long speech, spoken haltingly, ate up the little strength which otherwise might have permitted her to live another three hours.

Putting her hand on the boy's, which one of the Sisters had pushed slightly forward on the cover, Mercedes sighed, opened her eyes very wide as if she were seeing something amazing in the distance, moved her head slowly to the side where the boy stood—and was gone.

The Sisters now began in earnest to search for Mercedes' real son. He had to be somewhere. It was necessary to find him so that the authorities might take care of him and trace any relatives who could take him in.

Having taken full charge of Mercedes' affairs, the Sisters once again went to the little apartment in which Mercedes had lived during the last eight years.

Here everything was neat and clean. It contained all that a little boy of six would need. There was a photograph of the boy's mother and father, his mother wearing her wedding dress. Yet hard as they looked, no picture of the boy could be found anywhere.

An inquiry of the neighbors was made.

"Yes, of course, she had a boy. . . . No, we're new in this section, we've only recently moved here. . . . Yes, she had a boy. No, we've been living here almost a year now. . . . Now let me think, miss, to tell you the naked truth, no, I've never seen that kid of hers. I'm sure he must be staying with relatives. Perhaps he's still with them. Yes, a very fine and decent woman. A bit quiet. Very quiet I should say. Always tired from her work. . . . No, miss, never seen any male visitors

around. As decent a woman she was as the Lord makes. . . .
You're welcome."

The landlady, asked again, confirmed that Mercedes had
a boy, but she, too, had to admit that she had never seen him.
"Fact is," she added, "it's none of my business where the boy
might be hidden. She paid her rent punctually and always in
advance. That's all I care about. What my tenants do otherwise is their own affair."

The case was now turned over to the police, Missing
Persons Department.

The boy had to be located. However, no trace of him
could be found.

One of the detectives in charge of the case went to the
hospital and talked to the doctor who had attended Mercedes.

"Is there still a chance," the detective asked, "that a more
thorough examination of the young woman's body could be
made? What we want are certain particular examinations."

"Yes, officer?"

The detective whispered a few words into the doctors' ear.

"Of course, inspector, that examination can easily be
made. The body is still on ice; we've been waiting for any relatives who might claim it for burial. So far none has shown
up. I understand that the hotel girls she has been working with have taken up a collection so that together with
what the hotel management pays, she will have an extra fine
and decent burial."

"Good. Please have the examination made right away."

That had been in the morning.

In the afternoon of the same day, the Missing Persons
Department officer of the Police Department was called to the
telephone by the doctor in charge of Mercedes' case.

"Yes, this is Inspector Kinner talking. Yes, the same one
you saw this morning. Well, have you made that examination?"

"Yes, inspector, we have. She has never had a child.
What's more, she died still a virgin. No, inspector, not the
slightest doubt. No doubt at all. You're welcome."

Reviving the Dead *

"We must have twelve mules from the pasture," said Mr. Hilbert, the farmer, to Toribio, his foreman. "Tomorrow we want to start plowing up the tomato field. Ride up to the prairie and round up the twelve mules."

That was very early in the morning.

As Toribio was under way, he met the Indian boy Elfego. Elfego was eighteen and lived with his parents in the village. He had driven his cows to the prairie pasture and now was on his way home.

"Where are you riding to?" he asked Toribio.

"For my patron I have to round up twelve mules and bring them back. We need them for the plowing."

"That would really be fun for me to help you catch them," replied Elfego. "I don't have anything else to do now, anyway."

He turned his horse and rode with Toribio up to the American farmer's pasture. The pasture lay above the valley on a high plateau where also a man-made pond held enough water to supply the animals in the pasture. Mr. Hilbert had planted good guinea grass here; it made fine fodder for his

*Translated from the German
by Mina C. & H. Arthur Klein

cattle and for his mules and horses, which were driven up here to graze when there was no work for them to do in the fields below. The pasture was surrounded by dense primitive jungle. On its north side the pasture was bounded by a steep slope consisting of massive boulders.

Catching the mules would have been difficult for Toribio if he had not had Elfego to help, for the mules had not been worked for a long time and as a result had become somewhat wild. Finally they had assembled ten mules. Toribio had tied them together and he needed to round up only two more.

Toribio drove another mule toward Elfego. Elfego tossed his lasso far out in order to catch it. But with a sudden swerve the mule broke out from under the lasso and got away. Now Elfego tried to head off the mule and drive it toward Toribio, who covered the other semicircle, into which the mule had to run.

Elfego, riding like mad, had nearly driven the mule out of his semicircle and was trying to enlarge the curve by several lengths in order to take the mule from the rear by surprise. Suddenly, Elfego's horse, in the midst of its wildest running, jerked to a stop. The horse had suddenly discovered the rocky slope toward which Elfego had ridden too close because the high grass made him underestimate the distance to the slope. His horse's sudden jerking halt tossed Elfego head first over the saddle, his body still moving in the tempo of the wild gallop. He flew over his horse's head and over the edge of the slope. He did not fall far. Perhaps only three yards. But he struck head first and lay there unconscious.

Toribio had seen Elfego fly high over his horse's neck. But Toribio believed that this was just an ordinary fall such as often happens in riding, and he was convinced that Elfego had only fallen into grass, because Toribio, too, thought that the rocky slope did not reach to there. He was confident that Elfego, who knew the pasture well, was not careless enough to ride so close to the rocky slope. The truth is that Elfego had been carried away by the excitement of the round-up, and also was not to be blamed, because just at this point the rocky slope made a dip into the meadow with a notch hidden by the tall grass.

Toribio now directed his entire attention to the circling mule, which came charging toward him, believing itself still pursued by Elfego. Toribio threw his lasso, the lasso caught the mule, and Toribio then rode up to the panting animal, which by now stood still, in order to bring it over to the others and there tie it up until all twelve mules were ready to be driven off.

The high grass—higher in many places than a rider's head—prevented Toribio from seeing whether Elfego meantime had risen to his feet. As Toribio rode back, he saw a grazing mule near a large shady tree. Toribio dismounted, took his lasso, and cautiously slithered through the tall grass toward the grazing animal, getting so close to it that, even though not on his horse, he was able to lasso it. He now had all twelve mules together.

Toribio then whistled over toward Elfego. But no answer came. Then Toribio shouted, but this time, too, heard nothing in reply. Finally, he mounted his horse and rode to the place where he had seen Elfego fall. Elfego's horse stood quietly there and grazed.

Toribio reached the rocky dip and saw Elfego lying below him. He climbed down, picked Elfego up, and seated him upright on the stone. He shook Elfego, who after a while came to, disturbed and confused, as if awakened from a long sleep.

Toribio examined him but found no wounds. Then he asked, "Does anything hurt you, Elfego?"

"No," said Elfego, "nothing hurts me. My head hurts me a little. I think I have a bump."

Toribio examined his head but found no bump.

"Can you ride home?" asked Toribio.

"Yes, of course I can ride home."

Elfego stood up and climbed the rocky slope without needing help from Toribio. Toribio brought up their horses. Elfego put his foot in the stirrup, swung himself up, and was just about to seat himself in the saddle, when he said, "I feel bad and dizzy in the head. I'd better sit a while longer in the shade of that tree and rest a little."

"Good," said Toribio. "I'll sit with you over there. We

have time. Even if I don't get down with the mules until afternoon, it won't matter."

They both went over to the tree.

Here Elfego stood for a while, then reached out for the
tree trunk because he was afraid he would fall forward. At
this point, he shook his head as if it were connected loosely to
his neck; then he vomited hard, after which he sank to his
knees; finally he fell forward head first, shook while slowly
rolling onto his side, stretched out—and was dead.

Toribio shook him hard, pounded on the palms of his
hands, and on his pulse, as well as on his neck, but Elfego did
not come to. He no longer breathed and his heartbeat was no
longer audible.

Toribio pulled Elfego's handkerchief out of his pocket
and covered his face with it; then he raised the saddle on Elfego's horse, pulled out the sacks that served as a saddle-
blanket, and with them covered the corpse in order to keep
vultures away.

Then Toribio mounted his own horse. And once
mounted, he sat thinking for a while whether he should first
drive the twelve mules down or whether he had better ride
quickly to the village to tell Elfego's parents what had happened. After brief reflection, he decided to ride back at once
at the fastest trot, and later to drive down the mules, because
after all he would be riding up here again with Elfego's father
to show him where the boy lay.

Elfego's father was not at home. He was in the main town
of the district, negotiating with a wood dealer for a delivery.

Only the mother was at home. Elfego was her only child.
She cried out in a shrill scream.

The neighbors came at once, and several men and boys
then went to Mrs. Hilbert (wife of the American farmer), asking for the use of a light wagon with which they could ride
close to the mountain in order to bring the body home.

By three in the afternoon they were back again at the
village with the wagon and the body. At the entrance to the
village they halted. They quickly lashed together a stretcher-
like frame, laid Elfego on it, pulled a cover over him, and

thus in a solemn procession, all bearers and followers with
bared heads, carried him into his mother's house.

As they appeared at the barbed-wire fence that enclosed
the small premises of Elfego's parents, his mother cried out
piercingly, and all the neighboring women and women
relatives who were waiting in the victim's house, joined in
that piercing cry.

Elfego's mother had borrowed a table, placed it next to
her own, spread over them a white linen sheet, scattered flowers on them, placed at the head a large, crudely colored picture
of the Virgin Mary, and lit six candles which stood in front of
the picture.

The boy's body was laid on the tables, and his mother
threw herself on it.

The modest room in the thin-walled wooden house was
packed full of people. Mrs. Hilbert was there too and tried to
help or to calm the weeping mother.

It was probably just about this time when I rode up to
Mr. Hilbert's house, dismounted from my horse, went into
the house to ask Mr. Hilbert for several magazines, and
to chat with him for half an hour. We had been sitting
together a good while when Toribio came into the house and
told us what had happend. Until then Mr. Hilbert knew nothing about it, because he had only a short time before ridden
home from one of his distant fields, and his wife was, after all,
already at the boy's house. He had not asked the maids
where she was.

"Let's go over there and see what's happening," said Mr.
Hilbert.

We entered Elfego's house and found the whole village
gathered there. Those people who found no room inside the
house stood around outside. All of them had looked at the
corpse inside before they went outside again to stand around.
The women were endlessly busy, mostly with quite superfluous things, but they did it to show the mother that they stood
with her in order to render aid.

Mr. Hilbert and I, we went right up to the corpse and
looked closely at it.

"Just when did he die?" I asked. "What time?"

"This morning at about nine o'clock."

I looked at the clock.

"And now it is five."

I lifted the covering from the eyes of the dead boy, felt his cranium, pressed my fingers on his chest, took up his hands and moved their fingers.

Mr. Hilbert was standing behind me. I turned around to him and said, "This boy is not dead. He's still alive. He's supposed to have been dead since nine in the morning. That's eight hours ago. His fingers are just as flexible as mine and yours; his eyes are fixed, but not glazed as in death. Feel his cranium. Well? It's quite warm. If the lad had been dead for eight hours, then nothing would be warm any longer, and the fingers would be stiff already. Yesterday we had a heavy rain. Today was an unusually hot day. The lad ought to be stinking by now. But he isn't stinking. Not a trace of it."

"It seems, indeed, as if you are right," said Mr. Hilbert. "Let's get to work on him."

Elfego's mother who had been sitting listlessly in a corner, and only occasionally cried out piercingly, looked up now as I examined the lad so thoroughly and then spoke to Mr. Hilbert about the case.

"Give me a mirror," I said to one of the women. The mirror was brought, and I held it to the victim's mouth. A very faint film of mist was visible on the glass when I looked at the mirror.

While this was going on, everyone present, including the mother, had watched me constantly. They gave the impression of not venturing to breathe. Without doubt they expected that I would now take the boy by the hand and say to him, "Arise and walk!" whereupon he would walk. But I knew better than that.

I looked up now and said, "The boy is still alive; I suspect that he hears every word we are saying here. He has only a very severe concussion of the brain."

His mother jumped to her feet. She was about to cry out

for joy, but she controlled herself in time and pressed her hand against her mouth.

"Really," I added now, "it's impossible to say whether the boy will come to, or whether he will remain unconscious and die in spite of everything. That can't be predicted. It hangs in the balance."

"Tell us what we should do," whispered the mother. "We want to do whatever you think is right."

The mother busied herself and forgot all her suffering. From this moment on she regarded the boy simply as if he were someone sick with a fever who had to be given the most attentive care.

I ordered stones to be heated and placed against the soles of his feet. Then at the same time I had hot compresses applied to his body. Ice was brought from the market and I had ice applied to the top and back of his head. I said to myself, his head is still warm, so there must be a surplus of blood there, which we have to return to the rest of his body and feet, in order to get circulation started again.

We pounded or slapped on his pulse, pounded on his chest above the heart, and on his ankles and his feet. From time to time we performed artificial respiration. Ammonia was secured, and I held it under the boy's nose, and then I poured into his mouth several spoonfuls of strong brandy.

About two hours later, I talked to Mr. Hilbert who, in the meantime, had left but come back again, and to him I suggested opening an artery in the boy's pulse.

Such an arterial opening, perhaps, would start the blood flowing and reduce the blood congestion inside the boy's brain. There was no danger that too much blood would be lost, because we were right there and could bind off the upper arm with a tourniquet in plenty of time.

"It seems to me a very good idea," said Mr. Hilbert. "But I advise you not to do it. Even though his mother has said that she unconditionally entrusts her boy's body to you—if it goes wrong, the people can accuse you of having performed an operation, and the thing can be twisted in such a way that you stand accused of having killed the boy by opening the artery. That can become an unpleasant thing. As long as we work here just on the surface, with hot stones, compresses, and ice applications, it doesn't matter; but if you start cutting, then they can hang onto you something that you couldn't get rid of later."

That was good advice. You are an alien and you find yourself amidst an alien people that thinks and judges differently.

So I didn't open the artery.

By this time it was eleven o'clock at night. Some of the people had left, but their places were taken by others who had arrived from distant villages, either because they were passing through anyway, or out of curiosity.

Nothing about the victim had changed. His fingers and toes, like his arms and legs, remained flexible and movable. The eyes were not glazed as in death. His cranium remained warm, though not as warm as in the afternoon. His lips were blue with a rosy cast, and his fingernails were chalk-white, but if you pressed them very hard and then let go, they showed a very faint rosy tone. I held a burning match near his lower arm. The skin reddened slightly, but formed no blister.

I cooled the mirror with ice and held it in front of his slightly opened mouth. A scarcely visible film showed on the mirror. His eyelids were shut tight, and if they were lifted they closed slowly again after a while.

The boy was still alive. There was no doubt about it.

His brown face now had an expression quite different from that it had shown in the early afternoon. In the afternoon the face wore the rigid expression of a corpse. Now, on the contrary, the face had the expression of a person in a deep sleep, as if in a heavy, drugged stupor. You got the impression that the lad at any instant must open his eyes, an impression you did not have in the afternoon.

Among the new arrivals in the house was a Spaniard. I knew him. He was a charcoal buyer.

As soon as he stepped into the room, he began to act important. He tossed his hat into a corner, forced his way through the rest of the people, came to the victim, and took hold of him roughly as if to show that he alone knew how such a case should be treated. He was very noisy. The Spaniard's actions seemed uncommonly objectionable and pushy, because until now everything had been done very quietly—all the treatments, the changing of the hot stones and applications, as well as the constantly repeated artificial respiration and massages or poundings. True, they were energetic and positive, but always done silently or only with whispered accompaniment.

The Spaniard felt the victim's cheeks, lifted his eyelids, and then said very loudly and peremptorily, "He isn't dead. We'll have him up and around right away. What's being done here is all wrong. It's just the reverse of what's needed. The ice goes to the feet right away, and ice applications to his body. The hot stones have to be put on his head and neck."

The victim's mother till now had been doing willingly all I had ordered and had trusted my suggestions to the letter; now she stopped still in the middle of the room. She was just then carrying a hot stone in a piece of sackcloth in order to replace a stone that had grown cool against the feet. She became totally confused and looked at me with wide-open eyes to see what I had to say to this.

I shrugged my shoulders, stepped away from the boy and retreated into the background, leaving the field to the Spaniard. In this situation only the mother could decide whose instructions were to be followed.

I saw that she wanted to speak, and I felt that she would tell the Spaniard to be on his way. But the Spaniard left her no time to think or say anything. He almost tore the hot stone out of her hand, roughly grabbed the ice from the neck and from the top of the victim's head, laid it against the boy's feet, and pushed all the hot stones he could get under the neck and under the back of the head.

Now the mother stood motionless in the room. She paid no attention to anything more. She did nothing more. She became completely passive. All the excitement that she had experienced during twelve hours or more showed now quite suddenly in an exhaustion that she could no longer resist. The abrupt and brutal actions of the Spaniard affected her like a heavy blow that crippled her will, her hopes, and all her powers of resistance. She dragged herself to a chair in the corner of the room, sank into it, and collapsed completely.

The Spaniard worked loudly and noisily, barking out orders and constantly chattering around the victim. He altered everything—the legs had to be raised much higher than the head—and talked as if the poor lad would have been buried alive had not he, the Spaniard, fortunately come along. Mr. Hilbert and I had been standing at the rear during this time. Now that several people had left the room, we again approached the table on which the victim lay.

In the half hour during which we had not seen the body, something remarkable had happened. The expression on the face had changed completely.

The mouth had distorted itself into a peculiar ironic grin, expressing the entire unvarnished answer to the question, "D'you know what all of you can do, as far's I'm concerned?"

I looked at the lad for a while, then I gently nudged Mr. Hilbert. He saw it too. The lower jaw sank slowly and the lad's strong, healthy teeth protruded sharply.

That was around half past twelve at night. And I went home.

Next morning about eight I went back to Elfego's house. The house was empty; all its doors stood open. I went into the house of the nearest neighbor. I met there an old Indian woman who was squatting and smoking.

"Elfego?" said the woman. "Sure, don't you know? They've taken him to the cemetery. This morning around six he stank and his fingers were stiff, and so they left with him around seven. But this you know, Señor—the Spaniard murdered the poor boy."

This is the reason why, since then, in that village it is declared that I can awaken the dead, though until now I have never awakened even one dead person.

But the proof that I can awaken the dead is evident beyond all doubt in the opinion of these people. For even the simplest and most unassuming Indian will grasp this fact: If in every respect I do the exact opposite of that which kills a person, then the result must always be: a revival of the dead.

Accomplices *

Vicente Pliego couldn't make it any more in Jalisco, where he had already been involved with the police several times. He had to clear out now because a new director of police had been installed, who began quickly and thoroughly to clean out the lesser thieves and criminals. That didn't work so easily with the bigger thieves because some of them were members of the Police Director's own family, and others were Diputados who had enough influence to help oust the Police Director (if he caused them trouble). And because Vicente Pliego couldn't compete with the big boys, he removed himself from the spotlight for a while and went to Mexico City, where he was not yet known.

Vicente Pliego was a mestizo. Thievery was his regular line. He had never had any other profession and hoped never to be forced to undertake another.

In Mexico City he kept his head comfortably above water for a while by picking pockets. He was a good Catholic, and so did his best business inside the churches. He knelt piously, loaded with many crucifixes, next to kneeling and

*Translated from the German
by Mina C. & H. Arthur Klein

fervently praying women, and cleaned out their handbags. From the back pockets of kneeling men he extracted purses or wallets and relieved them of their timepieces. He regarded it as un-Catholic and shameless to rob the offerings-boxes of the churches—because that was successfully taken care of by others who were more skillful than he and who had threatened to knife him if he tried to trespass on the specialty that they regarded as their particular privilege.

Vicente got to know a girl, and because of her needed a big sum of money, for she demanded elegant clothes, gold earrings, bracelets, and other things a girl likes to have.

From a chauffeur he learned about a very well-to-do family that lived in one of the elegant avenues of the Condesa, and Vicente decided to get from this family the sum of money he needed. He paid a visit to his friend the chauffeur, during which he looked over the family's house, with the wise intention of learning the lay of the land.

All over Mexico are churches sheltering certain saints who have gained the reputation, based on long experience, of being friendly to thieves, burglars, street robbers, and robbers who also murder—saints reputed not to refuse their divine protection, provided of course that they have been sufficiently prayed to and that candles and other particularly fine metallic-sounding offerings have been laid at their feet. In addition, these saints expect that their renown will be proclaimed to the world. The unconsecrated and uninitiated person has no authority to deliver such eulogies to the saints either in public or even in church. Consequently, the simple believer is obliged to write a letter and in the letter to express his thanks to the saint for the help that has been given, mentioning what kind of help that was. This letter, open for every other believer to see, is fastened with a pin to the cowl or the velvet robe of the saint.

Near the Merced Market, Vicente had met a fortune-teller to whom he paid fifty centavos to find out from her which saint probably was most favorably disposed toward his particular deals. The fortune-teller was immediately wise to this customer—after all, would she otherwise have been a fortune-teller?—and she gave Vicente the name of the church and the name of the saint suited to his special needs. She told him in which niche to find the saint, how the saint looked, and how much money he would expect for his cooperation.

The church was near the Barrio de la Bolsa, that notorious section of Mexico City denounced as the world's most dangerous district because of robbers, murderers, and criminals. It is rated as even worse than any similar city section of New York, Chicago, San Francisco, London, or Paris. Strangers and tourists who visit Mexico City are always warned urgently not to visit that section either by day or night, because no guarantee at all can be given as to the safety of their money, or their clothing, including their shirts—and virtually no guarantee for their lives. Here is the usual place to hire murderers for political or private purposes.

And all the people who live here have their rosaries in their pockets and wear around their necks amulets blessed by the priests, and every day—without fail—they go at least once for ten minutes into one of the numerous churches of the district to sprinkle themselves with holy water and to genuflect before the Mother of God and to make their obligatory signs of the cross.

This part of the city is today rechristened so that tourists should not find it; but all travel guides still carry its former, correct name. A man occupying high office in Mexico, who obviously is not favorably disposed toward the Mexican proletariat and its heroic struggle for intellectual and economic freedom, has officially given the name "Avenue of Labor" to the main street in this notorious district; just as he gave the name "Colony of the Workers" to the filthiest district, in which not one street is paved, where there are neither sewers nor sanitation, and where, as a result, the most revolting excrement lies openly in the streets, and openly is added to at all times of day by men, women, and children, driven to do so by their bodily needs, because there is no other way available for them to dispose of their excrement.

One cannot, however, convert a girl into a boy by a

mere change of name alone. And so today, when inquisitive tourists in Mexico ask, "Where is the most notorious criminal district here?" they are given the honest answer, "It is the Avenue of Labor." And if the tourists ask, "Where is the filthiest, most neglected, and most stinking part of the city?" the truthful answer is, "It is the Colony of the Workers."

Thus is attained what that street-rechristener wanted to attain because of his hatred and contempt for the Mexican proletariat; and in this way he demonstrated that there are many effective methods by which conservative bureaucrats can successfully operate, even under a government that is honestly friendly to the workers.

Vicente at once went into action to make friends with his newly acquired saint. He found the saint obviously willing and ready not to withhold his celestial support. Vicente kneeled down and piously repeated all the prayers that the prayerbook provided for that saint, and explained his plans to him and in what form he, Vicente, expected cooperation.

"If everything goes good, if I come out right with all of it and am not nabbed, then I will give you twenty candles and twenty-five percent of the take," Vicente promised the saint in a whispered prayer.

Then he added a series of other prayers, placed four new candles on the altar, crossed himself, and left the church. He left with the conviction that he could now successfully commit the planned break-in, even if two policemen were to be standing in front of the house.

Two days later Vicente received news from his friend the chauffeur that he had to drive his employer's family to San Angel for a birthday celebration, and the family quite certainly would not be back home before two o'clock the following morning. The servants all had been given time off to go to the movies, and would not be back in the house before midnight.

Vicente pulled off the whole job alone, without any help.

The next morning found Vicente in possession of about twenty-four hundred pesos, two watches, several rings, a gold cigarette case, and several other trifles that usually have a way of showing up as bonuses in the course of such a visit.

All had gone well. A policeman had seen him leave the house, but had said nothing and surely suspected nothing. And because everything had gone so admirably and quietly and without a single shot fired, Vicente recalled the promise he had made to the saint.

He went to an "evangelist" in the colonnades of the Plaza de Santo Domingo, and had a letter of thanks to the saint written on a typewriter, and insisted that the most important parts of the letter be typed in red. The evangelist charged one peso extra for this, even though it caused him no extra work because the typewriter already had a black-and-red ribbon.

But Vicente could not take the letter to the saint right away, because he had a date with his girl, and this date prolonged itself more and more until finally it was too late to go out to that church. However, that same evening Vicente paid the agreed reward to his friend the chauffeur.

It was, finally, the following afternoon when Vicente once again recalled his duty to the saint. By this time, he discovered, his dates with his girl and the purchases connected with these dates, had cost him so much that he could in no way pay to the saint the promised twenty-five percent of the take —that is, about six hundred pesos—which should have been put into that saint's offerings-box.

True, Vicente still had about seven hundred pesos left, but if he gave six hundred of this to the saint, that would mean, beginning tomorrow, no more dates with his girl. Vicente reached the conclusion that the saint, after all, was most beneficent and abounding in great understanding of human weaknesses, and that he assuredly would be quite satisfied with two hundred pesos—perhaps even with one hundred and fifty pesos.

So the following afternoon Vicente went to the church, knelt down, took care of his prayers, fastened to the garments of the saint the handsome typed red-and-black letter of thanks, and began to insert the pesos—each a silver one-peso piece—one after another into the slit of the box for offerings. This took a good while to do.

He was not the only person kneeling before that saint, because there was more than just one thief in Mexico. The non-thieves, for their part, had other saints, according to their needs. Admittedly, the non-thieves often did not know for sure whether the projects for which they implored help from *their* saints shouldn't really belong more in the particular area of the saint that Vicente had selected for himself. . . .

Because Vicente was not the only one praying, he paid little attention to the others who were kneeling and praying to the same saint. He did see a man kneeling there who seemed to belong to Vicente's own trade. This man stood up and looked superficially at the letters of thanks attached to the garments on the image of the saint. The man seemed familiar with all the letters, because he noticed at once that a new letter had been added, and he had seen, too, who had added it. Moreover, he saw Vicente put one peso after another into the slit of the offerings-box. Having seen this, the man knelt down again and prayed with deep fervor, crossing himself innumerable times.

Vicente meanwhile had finished his payments to the saint. He had whittled away twenty pesos more from the reward, because it finally struck him as stupid to be pushing the beautiful pesos one after another into the box for so long.

Again Vicente knelt in order to make his final prayer. He streaked through it in a hurry because, just at this moment he recalled that he had previously made a date with his girl. The other man, who belonged to the same trade and who laid his affairs on the heart of the saint just as urgently as Vicente had done, was still kneeling. But now at last he seemed to be finished. He crossed himself again a number of times, then arose and left the church.

Outside, in front of the church, he beckoned to his side a man standing around there idly as if bored, smoking a cigar. The man carried a cane, but seemed not to know what to do with it, for he shifted it from one arm to the other, tossed it around in the air, held it like a rifle, then like a broom, then scratched around with it on the stones of the street, then rubbed it behind his ears—and whatever else one can do if, as a child, one hasn't learned that a cane has only one purpose: namely, that you can leave it behind somewhere and hurry away, so hopefully it won't be returned to you later on.

So this man was outside the church. He had a cane. And he smoked a cigar. People of this kind are the same all over the world. You can recognize them at two hundred paces, and you can recognize them more easily than policemen in uniform, concerning whom you often do not know whether they are leftovers from some costume ball, or are part of the new troop of guards that is to be dispatched to duty in the Upper Congo.

But—and this is the point—the man who likewise belonged in Vicente's trade, and who also knelt devoutly before the saint and crossed himself, understands how to read all the letters of thanks pinned to the saint's plush robe, and understands how to read them far better than the cleverest thief with the aid of the best "evangelist" ever will be able to write them. The thief in his letter must at least indicate, however ambiguously and guardedly, what the saint has done for him, because otherwise the saint won't know what it is all about, and he mixes up the letters, the money, and the names, and —from sheer oversight—extends aid, not to the one who has paid most money and written the most beautiful letter of tribute, but rather to the one who has behaved most shabbily with regard to the candles, the letter of praise, and the money.

The police, no less than the thieves, pray to the saint. And when the police receive a report that the night before a particular house has been broken into, and this and that stolen, and the thief is still at large, then a policeman in plain clothes goes to the Volador, the thieves' market, where stolen goods are traded. Another policeman visits certain churches, all of whose saints he knows well.

If the thief has not been caught, he'll appear to give thanks to his saint—if not today, then tomorrow or the day after. But appear he will, because he is a good Catholic, believing in the willingness of his saints to give help, and feeling obliged to thank them.

The chauffeur had been arrested the day before, because the police, though they may be very stupid, are not so stupid that they fail to know after a few hours that someone who belonged to the burglarized house must have told someone who didn't—told them when the house was going to be empty and where the cash could be found.

And Vicente, the true believer, had written in his letter of thanks in red, and couched in a trusting and comradely style of address:

> ". . . and I kiss you Santito mio, my little saint, on your heart in gratitude for sending me so good a friend as my friend the Ch————r Pancho L. And from the depths of my heart I beg you to protect him too and to heap your blessings upon him, and I glorify. . . ."

Even if the police have no interest in whether thieves are caught or not (the money being, in any case, gone), still they cannot permit such a letter to be displayed right in front of their noses and say, so to speak, "We're sorry to have made a big mistake by arresting the chauffeur!"—not if the police have a spark of professional pride. Policemen and judges commit no errors. If someone is executed and later it is revealed that he had been innocent of the crime for which he lost his life, then it was his own fault: why had he put himself so near to the scene of the crime that one was bound to believe him guilty? When a crime is committed, you should get out of the area in good time; then you, as an innocent person, can never be arrested.

All these very wonderful researches and considerations and deep thoughts about the administration of justice were familiar neither to Vicente nor to his faithful friend the chauffeur. Next time, both of them would do the very same things—again write letters to the saint and again kneel before the saint.

It soon became clear to them why the holy saint had let them down.

Vicente and the chauffeur met in the Belén prison. Neither had squealed on the other. They were even better friends now than they had been before.

"I don't understand," said the chauffeur, "why your saint left you in the lurch so completely."

"I know why," said Vicente gloomily. "I got out of the house in great shape. But dammit, then I did a real dumb thing. I had promised the saint twenty-five percent. D'you know, Chato, how much I actually gave him? Eighty pesos —and even from that I took off twenty pesos more. And I didn't bring him the twenty candles either."

"Well, then, frankly," said the chauffeur, "I'm not surprised any more that we're sitting here now. For that kind of money he couldn't take care of it, not even with the best intentions. You really should have known that. If I, in his place, wouldn't have done it for so little, how can you expect it from your Santo?

"Such a blockhead as you, I haven't seen in a long time!"

Indian Dance in the Jungle *

For several months I had lived in a primitive hut in the jungle. To get to the next settlement where a white family lived I had to ride about three hours. All the people in my vicinity were Indians. But even the nearest of them was half an hour's ride from my place.

It was a late afternoon in November, near the end of the month, and very hot. I sat half-naked in front of my hut and read. All at once, an Indian, my nearest neighbor, rode up in an easygoing way, sat down next to me, and we talked for a while about all the work that was waiting for us to do. Allegedly waiting, because really none of us did any of it—neither the Indian nor I.

Following this preamble about lots of work and little money for it, my neighbor got around to the real point of his visit.

"Señor," he said laughing, "tonight we're holding a dance. We have musica, muy bonita, and I too will play beautifully, guitarra. I've learned it five days."

*Translated from the German
by Mina C. & H. Arthur Klein

By that he meant that he'd begun just five days earlier to learn to play the guitar.

"We're going to have a lot of fun," he continued. "You're here so alone and so very sad, Señor. . . ."

I wasn't a bit sad; quite the contrary. I was quite happy not to be hearing streetcars, autos, or ringing telephones. But if you don't take an Indian woman into your hut as cook, then, in the opinion of the Indians, you are sad beyond all doubt. True enough. But I couldn't produce the eight pesos a month that a cook would want as wages.

"That's why I would like to invite you, Señor. Come over to our dance; you can eat supper at my place."

"Will pretty girls be coming?" I asked.

"Señor dammitall, the very prettiest who live around here!"

Right after sundown I set out. If I didn't want to try to find my way through the bush in the raven-black night, I had to hurry, because once the sun vanishes on the horizon, you have just barely time to turn around and night is upon you without your being able to say how it got there so swiftly.

My neighbor's hut was on the same mountain-chain as my bear-den of a hut, but he lived even farther off the beaten paths and deeper into the thickets. Why he had withdrawn himself so far is another story.

The place was idyllic. About a dozen gigantic ebony trees were scattered around his jungle clearing that formed a sort of plateau from which one could look far out over the level jungle land. These noble trees did not stand there like indifferent columns. With the long gray beards of moss hanging from their branches, they gave the impression of being aged but very jolly gentlemen, waiting there with much pleasure for the dance to begin.

Two Indians and their wives were already there. After the very polite greetings were over, I was invited to come into the hut and have supper. There were black beans, tortillas, and coffee.

Meanwhile more guests arrived, all Indians. I was the only white person and probably was invited merely because I was a fellow-resident of this wild jungle district. The Indians came riding on horses, mules, or donkeys. Many had no saddles. All brought their wives and children. Sometimes husband, wife, and two children sat on the same horse, while the wife held a nursing infant in her arms. In bags of woven bark they brought tortillas in case they should get hungry, for the dancing continues till dawn.

The women carried in sacks their flimsy muslin dresses and low patent-leather shoes. They arrived either barefoot or wearing simple homemade sandals, and had on their cheap cotton dresses.

As soon as they had dismounted, assisted in a courteous manner by their husbands, they withdrew into a corner of the reed hut or behind it and changed their clothes. They washed themselves again, using soap that smelled strongly of patchouli and musk. Then they let down their long raven-black hair and combed it carefully.

The moon had come up, a round, shining, ripe full moon. And it glided in majestic calm over the vibrantly clear night sky.

By and by the women came forward shyly, smoothing down the folds of their thin garments. Their dresses were short, in keeping with the style, had short sleeves, and exposed their throats and necks. Into their unbound hair they had fastened flowers. Some of the women were hardly fifteen or sixteen, yet already had their infants with them. All the other women, who had no infants, were expecting them soon.

The host of the dance had laid several boards over a couple of rotting wooden chests so the ladies could sit down. The men stood around chatting. They had not changed their clothes, because they had nothing to change into. They wore their usual yellow or blue coarse cotton trousers, white or colored cotton shirts, sandals or shoes, and their big, pointed, high-crowned straw hats. Jackets or vests they did not have. In place of these, some had brought along brown, red, or multicolored woolen blankets, in case it should grow cool during the night.

The women had big black cotton scarves that they wore around their shoulders. These scarves serve as hat, as veil, as

warm muffler, as shawl, often as handkerchief, and sometimes even as nursing baby's diaper; and, when folded, as a
head pad for heavy jugs of water that have to be carried up
from streams.

The musicians also had had their black beans and coffee.
Then they rolled themselves cigarettes, and when these had
been smoked, the music began. One violin and one guitar. My
neighbor wasn't playing yet; he wanted to dance first.

He had a handsome wife, pure full-blooded Indian. She
was the best-dressed of all the women, with flowers which she
had placed very tastefully in her hair. Besides, she had per-
fumed herself. She was not quite twenty years old. Her eldest
son, about five years of age, revealed himself during the night
to be an excellent solo dancer, and a consumer of at least
twenty cigarettes. His mother was the only one who did not
smoke among all the women, men, girls, and children present.
Every other human being past the age of six smoked like mad.

If only one-fifth of what the nonsmokers and anti-nico-
tine fanatics say about the damage done by smoking were
true, then the Indian race would have long ago died out, gone
blind, or insane; for the Indians have been smoking tobacco an
estimated eleven thousand years longer than all other peoples.

As soon as the music began, the dancing started. Of the
hesitations that often make the first hour of a dancing party
seem like a funeral ceremony, these people know nothing. For
them, dancing is not a seduction by Beelzebub, and even less
is it something contrary to the dignity of a human being.
Women were there with their children and also with their
grandchildren who themselves were already pregnant. Meanwhile, the about-to-be great-grandmother herself still had a
nursing infant at her breast. And this defiantly vital great-
grandmother danced no less often and no less gracefully than
the fifteen-year-old girls.

The women nursed their infants without showing any
prudery or shame. It took place so naturally, so openly, as if a
bottle of milk were being given to the baby. When the little
ones had drunk their fill, they were wrapped in a black cotton

scarf and laid flat on the ground, right under the bench, but pushed back a little so the heels of the dancers' shoes would not touch them. The babies then slept contentedly and steadily until about midnight, when they made themselves heard, and again found their mothers' two milk containers filled, even though she had not missed a single dance in the meantime.

If you know from experience what crawls around on the ground at night in the tropical jungle—even in an illuminated clearing like this one—then you get ice-cold chills to see the little infants bedded down there.

The older children played for a while, then got tired, laid themselves down on the bare earth beside the infants, pulled their knees up as high as possible, and slept like little rats. If their father had a blanket along, it was pushed under the child who was wrapped up like a tree trunk—until the next-older brother or sister came along, tired too, and was wrapped up along with the first sleeper.

More guests continued to ride up until about nine o'clock. It made an uncanny impression on me when suddenly in the midst of the music and dancing, a woman—or, less frequently—a man, would pause a few seconds, seem to be listening into the night, and then would say, "Here comes another couple. Who can they be?"

The path to this clearing led in long, heavily overgrown curves through the thick jungle. Even by day from the best lookout point you could see no one more distant than about three hundred yards. As a result of the music and the conversation, you could hear nothing that took place beyond a short distance.

When someone said, "A couple is coming on a mule," at least ten minutes, or often longer, passed before the announced arrivals could be seen. This gift of clairvoyance is even more developed among tribes that live farther south, and has a truly uncanny effect.

The musicians played entirely by ear. From time to time the fiddler would switch to playing the guitar and the guitarist to the fiddle. When a musician wanted to dance, one of the

Indians would take up his instrument and play, perhaps not quite so well as the musicians—who were, naturally, not professionals—but as well as all the rest of the Indian woodchoppers and charcoal burners.

My neighbor also hastened to demonstrate what he had learned in five days. I knew he had his guitar no longer than that because I had seen him bringing it home after he had borrowed it. Somebody had shown him how it should be held, shown him a few finger-positions, and that was all. What he now gave out was really amazing. True, he had only to provide accompaniment for the fiddle, but even that must be mastered. A couple of times he probably did make mistakes, but always found his way back to the right tone by himself.

The fiddler, a small, slender lad, danced rather seldom with the girls. He preferred to perform grotesque solo dances. These solo dances were so primitively comic that they not only made the Indians laugh until they seemed about to burst, but I, too, had to laugh so hard that my sides hurt.

The art of the dance can't be described—and even less so that of such grotesque dances.

American one-steps and foxtrots were played; also waltzes, which were danced here like the old-fashioned polkas, only much more slowly, similar to the so-called "Boston." The round-waltz, or Viennese waltz, is quite unknown here. They also danced a sort of "Rheinlaender." These dances had little interest for me.

However, about every fourth dance was what I wanted to see—an original dance. I have seen birds doing the same sort of dance in their mating seasons. They dance then in the same manner, displaying themselves before each other, which is uncommonly funny.

During the dance, the Indian couples alternately approach and then retreat from each other, but never touch, not even with their hands. At certain intervals the music stops and the musicians, as well as the men who are dancing without women partners, replace the music with singing. This singing is done at the highest range of the human voice and is a very rhythmical, yet shrill and screeching modulation of tones that have hardly any human quality. (The battle-cry of the Aztecs was a very high, shrill cry which filled the Spaniards with terror the first time they heard it.) A trace of terror overcomes you even when this singing is done for purely pleasurable purposes. Only in the case of this dance, and not otherwise, did I feel I was living in another world, that centuries divided me from my own time, and thousands of miles from my own race; that I was living on another planet than the one on which I had been born.

The moon now stood high over me. The tropical night sky was as glisteningly clear as a great black pearl. A white shimmering radiance lay like a flowing thin silken veil on the plateau, and it lay like a twinkling fog of light on the wide jungle. It was the dazzling radiance of day, hidden in a thick white cloud. Myriads upon myriads of grasshoppers, crickets, and tiny beetles sang the eternally ancient, unchanging song of the tropical night, while in the nearby bush and in the jungle, merciless struggles for life and love were fought.

A light wind stirred the gray beards of the ebony trees, and it was as if these old gentlemen, hundreds of years old, nodded to one another and told one another amusing things.

The tethered horses pawed the earth and sniffed, while the donkeys nibbled off poor dried-up stalks, chewed, and now and again brayed plaintively to frighten away the tigers who were creeping through the jungle.

Now and again a pig ran between the legs of the dancers, while another scratched its back on a wooden saddle that lay on the ground, and a third, grunting comfortably, wallowed in the mud formed where coffee dregs had been poured out.

A baby began to cry softly, and its mother let go of her dance partner, ran to the tiny bundle that was rolling on the ground, picked it up, unwrapped it, unbuttoned her dress, seated herself on the bench, and nursed the baby while she watched the dancers with amusement.

Every dance was played until the dancers were so exhausted that they had to lead their women partners to the bench. Only water was drunk, and that in large quantities. Two boys constantly had to run with a pail to a rainwater pool which lay in the jungle, and which at nighttime attracted all kinds of dangerous guests who were driven to it by thirst.

And I danced and danced. The younger women and girls were at first a little shy toward me, but they gained confidence when they saw that I did not bite and that I moved my legs in dancing just like the men of their tribe; also that I wore only trousers, shirt, and hat, and passed out my cigarettes. Soon I was able to do the Indian dance, which made the people wonder more than a little. True, I was not able to sing in the Indian style, and never will learn how; to do that, long practice is necessary, which, in the case of the masters, has lasted ten thousand years.

Soon I had discovered the best dancer among the women, and during the second half of the night I chose her, with few exceptions, for dance after dance—which no one seemed to hold against me. She was the great-grandmother. Her face was blackish-brown leather, wrinkled and creased; her eyes were black; her long, wispy hair was still blacker; and her skin gave off a sharp, pungent odor. Possibly if you encountered her in Central Europe you would take her for the Devil's grandmother. But she danced like a goddess, and her grace and charm as she danced were of great beauty.

Sunrise subdued the moon, subdued the music. Unobtrusively one woman after another withdrew behind the hut, coming out again after a while clad in her rags and carrying a little bundle. Just as unobtrusively, without farewell scenes, they mounted their horses and donkeys and vanished without a sound.

The risen sun found a bare clearing on which it seemed no one had ever danced or perhaps even dreamed of dancing.

PART II

In the Freest State

in the World

Introduction *

to IN THE FREEST STATE IN THE WORLD
by Mina C. and H. Arthur Klein
Marut/Traven in Germany, 1916-1922

In November, 1915, an obscure actor, after years in provincial German theaters, arrived in Munich, Bavaria. The small, slender, retiring man, who looked to be about thirty, brought along but little baggage. Ret Marut, as he generally called himself at the time, had no apparent prospects for roles in the theaters still operating in the Bavarian capital. German stages were greatly restricted, for the First World War had been under way more than a year, and already was hardening into a holocaust without victory or solution in sight.

By early 1916 he was settled in a modest corner room three flights above the ground floor, in an apartment house at 84 Clemens Strasse. A friend who had met him as an actor in Berlin, in 1910, recalled long afterward that when Marut came to Munich his suitcase held mostly manuscripts. They were not, however, the parts he had played since he first began acting on the German stage around 1908. Marut's manuscripts and his favorite books (many in English) were scattered around the tables and chairs in his room. Its walls were hung with astronomical drawings.

Marut's neighbors found him pleasant, quiet, and seri-

*(See also the notes following *In the Freest State in the World*)

155

ous. Often his typewriter hammered away until far into the night. Frequently he was accompanied or visited by a *Fräulein,* aged about twenty, and a trifle taller than he. The caretaker at 84 Clemens Strasse understood that they "worked for a periodical, or some such thing."

This, as well as most of the rest that can now be pieced together about Marut in Munich, we owe to an extraordinary literary researcher, historian, and dectective, Dr. Rolf Recknagel of Leipzig, Germany. But for Dr. Recknagel's dogged labors under great difficulties, the mysteries about Marut, deep as they are, would be far deeper still. Recknagel's work proved that this Ret Marut, ex-actor, aspiring writer, revolutionary editor, and cryptic activist, had metamorphosed fantastically, within the following decade, into B. Traven of Mexico, the no less mysterious teller of great stories—a figure for world literature to esteem and remember.

In 1965 appeared Recknagel's book, *B. Traven: Beiträge zur Biografie* (Contributions toward the Biography), presenting the mosaic of evidence he had patiently pieced together to demonstrate the Marut-Traven identity. Traven, then still living in Mexico City, denied, directly or otherwise, any connection with that earlier Ret Marut of Munich. But after Traven died in March, 1969, his widow, Rosa Elena Lujan, at his instructions revealed that he had indeed once been that Ret Marut.

The appearance of Marut/Traven as a journalist and writer begins with his militant, ultrapersonalized journal, *Der Ziegelbrenner,* the "periodical, or some such thing," on which he and his girl friend slaved during those wartime months and years in Munich. Its title means the brick-burner or brick-maker. It was published from Munich starting with the autumn of 1917 and continuing until certain catastrophic events early in May, 1919. Thereafter it appeared irregularly from elsewhere until 1922.

One must wonder still how the *Ziegelbrenner,* considering its content, could get past the German wartime censorship during the first five issues, written before the shooting phase of World War I ended in November, 1918. Its thrust, from the start, was aimed against the imperialist and capitalist establishment in Germany and the world.

One of Marut's few friends from those days recalled years later that, when offered for sale in the bookshops, the *Ziegelbrenner* had "struck like a bomb into the citadel of the press, which had grown tame and subservient to the wartime censorship. Marut," he went on, "with a boldness till then regarded as impossible, broke through all censorship limitations. He became the democratic wolf amid the flock of cowed sheep of the wartime press, the courageous spokesman for human rights amidst the timorous ranks of propagandists for war-bonds."

Marut wrote most of what appeared in its closely packed, neatly printed pages. His sole collaborator was Irene Mermet, the *Fräulein* already referred to. Like Marut she had "graduated" from the provincial stage, where she had acted under the names of Irene Alda and Aldor, into critical and political journalism. Together they prepared the editorials, comments, reviews, and exhortations which, almost unaccompanied by paid advertising, made the *Ziegelbrenner* exceptional then and memorable even now.

Yet even then Marut's life was enveloped in mystery. A keen observer from those distant days in Munich stressed later that "no one knew what his real name was, not even his girl friend [Mermet] was said to have been told."

A Novelist Also

Besides his numerous articles, Marut had also written and published what he called (in the *Ziegelbrenner*'s columns) a "master novel," the title of which was *An das Fräulein von S.* (To Miss von S.). True, its author was listed as Richard Maurhut, but even then there was little doubt that this was but another name for Marut.

The *Ziegelbrenner* was issued on only thirteen different dates. Marut had informed his subscribers from the start that the magazine would be published irregularly, as conditions permitted or his decisions dictated. The first three issues appeared at intervals of about three months. Then came a gap of eight months, filled with upheavals in the political and social life of Germany, especially in Bavaria.

Bearing the date of November 9, 1918 (but reaching regular subscribers by mail a week or two before that), a historic issue of 46 pages appeared. Its front cover was emblazoned with a jubilant and prophetic title: *Es dämmert der Tag* (The Day Is Dawning). By that date the ancient Kingdom of Bavaria had become a Republic under Socialist leadership. Two issues later the *Ziegelbrenner*'s lead editorial was headed triumphantly: "The World Revolution Begins." However, the following issue, dated March 10, 1919, proved to be its last appearance before counterrevolutionary terror triumphed in Munich. Marut's own recollections of how that terror entered his life appear in the following pages, as *In the Freest State in the World*.

After his extraordinary escape at the last moment, as therein described, Marut was a fugitive and hunted man. Bavarian police warrant No. 4236 had been issued for his arrest. On the "wanted" lists circulated in Germany his name appeared as a "ringleader" during the Council Republic of Bavaria, his offense being listed as "Member of the Ministry of Propaganda." The documents listed his birthplace as San Francisco, on February 25, 1882, and gave his parents' names as William and Helene Marut. If apprehended, Marut faced almost certain conviction, followed by a long imprisonment, or even possibly a death sentence. Anyone less stubborn and audacious would have dropped the *Ziegelbrenner*. Yet he managed somehow to produce five more issues illegally and to mail them out from various places during a two-year period, between December, 1919 and December, 1921. Where these extraordinary "fugitive" issues were printed remains uncertain, even now.

Why in Munich, Bavaria?

Bavaria had been an independent kingdom until less than half a century before the *Ziegelbrenner* appeared. With the unification of Imperial Germany, Bavaria became part of the Reich headed by the Hohenzollern Kaiser, but still retained its ancient ruling family, the Wittelsbachs, compared with whom the Prussian Hohenzollerns seemed like aggressive upstarts of royalty. Even under the Empire, strongly Catholic Bavaria was granted some autonomous rights. It maintained diplomatic relations with the Vatican and had its own army, educational system, taxation, and courts.

Bavaria's population of roughly seven million amounted to less than 11 percent of the total in the Kaiser's Reich. Prussia, by contrast, comprised some 60 percent. Moreover, most Bavarians were not overfond of their Prussian neighbors. When the First World War began in late summer of 1914, Bavaria's three army corps marched to the fray, like the other 20 army corps of the Reich. At first, enthusiasm and expectation of swift victory were widespread. But as the war dragged on, disaffection spread more rapidly in Bavaria than in most other parts of the Reich. More and more the holocaust seemed to be a nightmare, made in Prussia.

Bavaria as a whole was much less industrialized than Prussia and the Rheinland-Ruhr. Its population was weighted more heavily toward small tradesmen, handicraft workers, farmers and peasants. More than seventy percent of Bavarians were Catholic. This was reflected politically by the preponderant influence of the Bavarian Center (Catholic) Party. Yet beginning with the 1890's, socialist ideas had made headway, and the reforms called for by the Socialist Party of Germany (SPD) gained support from growing numbers of urban industrial workers, especially in the Munich area, as the terrible war dragged on and on, exacting an increasing toll in blood and money. Growing hunger, discontent, and despair led to strikes, demonstrations, and the erosion of old illusions and loyalties. The ruling Wittelsbach monarch, King Ludwig III of Bavaria, lacked charisma and energy.

During 1918 the influence of the new Independent Socialists (USPD) had increased in Bavaria. These Socialists actively called for peace and opposed the support given the war by the leaders of the Majority Socialists (SPD). As the winter of 1918 approached, vast numbers of Bavarians were in no mood to go on as before, although most orthodox political leaders either could not or would not realize this fact.

The Old Order Is Sloughed Off

Came a Thursday, November 7, mild and clear, good weather for an outdoor antiwar meeting that had been called at Munich's Bavaria Park. Crowds of workers from the local war factories were on hand, and among them were a number of soldiers, who had defied orders to keep to their barracks. Various orators addressed the crowd. Erhard Auer, the leading Majority Socialist, invited his listeners to a peace parade through the streets of Munich. But the star that afternoon proved to be a small, bearded intellectual, Kurt Eisner, an Independent Socialist, who had some years before been editor of the *Vörwarts,* official Socialist newspaper published in Berlin, and had initiated the Independent Socialist movement in Bavaria after the outbreak of the war. Eisner urged the soldiers to take over their barracks, arm themselves with the weapons there, and bring out with them the rest of the troops —so as to control their government and their own destiny. The crowd followed Eisner.

At a nearby munitions depository they collected guns, then moved on to the large Maximilian Barracks. Before evening these armed rank-and-file soldiers controlled the Munich garrisons. Red flags flew now, replacing the traditional blue and white banner of the Wittelsbach kingdom, and the black-white-red flag of the Hohenzollern Reich.

At the biggest beer hall of Munich, Eisner then conferred with the first Council of Workers and Soldiers, and was confirmed by them as the head of a new "Republic of Bavaria." Rapidly Eisner rounded up a cabinet, including three other Independent Socialists, three Majority Socialists, and one nonparty person. Before the end of the following day this new government held almost every key point in Munich, including its War Ministry building. In proclaiming the Bavarian Republic, Eisner designated as its supreme authority the newly formed Council of Workers, Soldiers, and Peasants.

Meanwhile, Ludwig III, last of the Wittelsbach kings, had fled. His private troops had joined the revolutionaries, and his famed old palace, known as the *Residenz* of Munich, was now being toured by hundreds of uninvited and curious citizens of the new "Republic." Thus the German "Revolution" of 1918 began—not in Berlin, but in Munich. Two days later, on November 9, amidst a general strike, the Reich Chancellor, Prince Max of Baden, announced that Kaiser Wilhelm II had abdicated. This was not at the moment literally true, but it became, so to speak, a self-fulfilling prophecy.

Leaders of the Majority Socialist Party, headed by Friedrich Ebert, then appeared at the Chancellery and informed Prince Max that the troops in Berlin were on their side. They urged that, in the interests of law and order, members of their party should now be given the highest offices. Prince Max consented, without too much hesitation. Later, Ebert's associate, Philipp Scheidemann, shouted news of the takeover to crowds gathered near the German Reichstag building in Berlin. On his own, seemingly in a slip of the tongue, he added, "Long live the German *Republic!*" The crowd roared approval. Ebert was enraged when he heard of this blunder, as he deemed it to be. He had expected and, apparently, preferred to become Chancellor of the existing Reich (Empire), not of a new Republic. But obviously most Germans were in no mood to turn back.

Thus, almost by inadvertence, the Hohenzollern Reich was ended and the rocky road of history detoured toward the Republic. Not long afterward it was to become known widely as "the Weimar Republic," and endured, amidst hair-raising difficulties and dissensions, until, soon after the start of 1933, Adolf Hitler dismantled it and converted it into a Fascist dictatorship.

Would Kaiser Wilhelm II have been forced to abdicate and flee after November 9 if the Bavarian King had not been toppled bloodlessly by Eisner a couple of days earlier? Perhaps the upset in Berlin would have been delayed and followed a somewhat different course. . . . In any case, beyond argument is the fact that the Bavarian overthrow became the initial step in Germany's "Revolution," and the further fact that about six months later, again in the Bavarian capital, a grim last act of that now aborted Revolution was performed, with Ret Marut as an active member of the cast.

That agitated half year was crowded with plans and changes, demands and decisions, rhetoric and acts of violence. Some of them must be sketched here to deepen our understanding of what Marut meant by his bitter and memorable protest-report: *In the Freest State in the World.*

Secret Ties to the Generals

Scarcely had Ebert become head of the provisional government in Berlin than he and General Groener, spokesman for the General Staff of the Army, came to a secret understanding. The generals would keep hands off, not seeking to overthrow the new regime; it in turn would not tolerate "Bolshevism." In practice this meant no socialization of industry or agriculture, and no effective control by the working class. It meant a Germany basically unaltered, though superficially the forms of government had shifted.

This deal was clandestine; however the policies of the Ebert government increasingly infuriated the radicalized workers of Berlin and other urban centers. Demonstrations and strikes pressed radical demands, including one for full recognition and power to the Councils of Workers and Soldiers that had been widely formed. By early January, 1919, Ebert and his group were fearful, even desperate. They now deliberately sought by force of arms to crush these dissidents. For this they needed someone at the top who would work with the Army chiefs in organizing and directing a final suppression of the "reds."

The Majority Socialists' specialist on military matters was Gustav Noske. In the Reichstag for years he had supported military budgets, and worked against the demands of pacifists or antimilitarists in or out of his party. Early in January, Ebert hastily offered Noske the "defense" post in the hard-pressed provisional government. There were no illusions on either side. Noske accepted at once, with a remark both knowing and cynical: "It's all right with me. Somebody's got to be the bloodhound. I don't dodge that responsibility. . . ."

Noske moved rapidly. Well-armed forces drawn both from the remnants of the regular army and from newly gathered irregulars or *Freikorps* were thrown into action. They crushed radical groups, especially the Spartacists, capturing or killing their leaders and guard units. In Berlin, the terror raged from January 8 to 12. It ended with the elimination of the principal officials of the new German Communist Party, formed only a few days earlier, and the wrecking of its offices. On January 15, its two outstanding leaders, Karl Liebknecht and Rosa Luxemburg, were captured and brutally murdered by counterrevolutionary soldiers.

By January 19 an effective revolutionary movement had been wiped out in major centers throughout most of Germany. That, significantly, was the date set for a nationwide election of delegates for a national assembly, which in February was scheduled to establish a regular government, and frame for the nation a new, republican constitution.

In quasi-autonomous Bavaria, meanwhile, the Eisner regime still limped along, well-meaning, kindly, somewhat quixotic and chaotic—but with no ties to the Army high command or the ultraconservatives. Two elections took place in Bavaria, just a week apart. The first, January 12, chose a new state legislature *(Landtag)*. The next, January 19, was part of the general election for the National Assembly.

The Ebert regime in Berlin had ordained that, for the first time in German history, women as well as men were to have the right to vote—and that the voting age was to be reduced to 20, instead of the former 25. Much as Ret Marut predicted in his writings prior to those elections, they resulted in setbacks for the radicals.

On January 12, Eisner's Independent Socialists (USP), polling a mere 80,000 votes, got only three seats in the new legislature. The Catholic Center, now called the Bavarian People's Party (BVP) won 58 seats—losing their former domination, but remaining the strongest single party. The Majority Socialists (SPD) won 52 seats, the Peasant Union 16, and the National Liberals 5. Clearly, once the new Bavarian *Landtag* was called into session, it would bring the Eisner government to an end. For the time being, however, it was not summoned to meet.

The January 19 elections throughout Germany chose 421 delegates to the National Assembly. Of these 39 percent (163) were Majority Socialists (SPD), 5 percent (22) were Independent Socialists (USPD), and both these Socialist parties together had only 44 percent, well below a clear majority. Together, the various parties of the Center and Right could claim a majority. It was no accident that Ret Marut, surveying the electoral catastrophe in the article that follows, began with an attack on the election and voting system which had led to such setbacks for the causes he supported. He had long warned that the hasty grant of the franchise to women might mean that many of them would vote as their father confessors urged or indicated they should.

Early in February the National Assembly gathered at Weimar, safely insulated from the radicalized capital, Berlin. By February 11, its delegates had designated Ebert as the first President of the new Republic of Germany. He in turn chose as his Chancellor, Philipp Scheidemann. And to the surprise of none but the indignation of some, the first cabinet minister of the Army became—Gustav Noske. By now Noske was well on his way to being perhaps the politician most hated by the extreme left—anarchist-minded individualists like Marut as well as Communists and Independent Socialists. By the time Marut wrote the piece that follows, the name Noske inspired fury among radicals.

Murder in Munich

On February 21, Kurt Eisner, still Premier of Bavaria, was on his way to open the new *Landtag* for the first time. He was in fact about to announce his resignation, since the Bavarian elections had failed to support him. But Eisner never arrived. He was shot down by a 22-year-old student, Count Arco-Valley, a reactionary aspirant who hoped thus to demonstrate his fitness for membership in an anti-Semitic and fascist-like group calling itself the Thule Society. This vicious act of murder triggered resentment, reprisals, and attempts to take revenge. Later that day in the *Landtag* an Eisner supporter fired on the Majority Socialist leader, Erhard Auer, wounding him seriously and killing an officer from the Bavarian Ministry of War who had tried to save Auer. A member of the Catholic Party (BVP) was killed also in the confusion.

Revolt flared in Bavaria. It climaxed in a general strike, in seizure of newspaper offices, and in establishment of a Central Council representing the separate Councils of Workers and Soldiers active in Munich and elsewhere. The Bavarian *Landtag* managed in March to put together a new government with a Majority Socialist as premier: Johannes Hoffmann, a schoolteacher. However, the Central Council and its supporters rejected the Hoffmann government and finally, on April 4, ordered the *Landtag* itself to cease meeting or legislating. Three days later the Central Council proclaimed a Republic of Councils, or Council Republic *(Räte-Republik)* for Bavaria. This new regime rejected cooperation with what they called the shameful, despicable "Ebert-Scheidemann-Noske" government in Berlin.

A new Bavarian government was named, composed of "people's representatives," none of whom had supported the Hoffmann cabinet. Independent Socialists and anarchists were included among these people's representatives. Now Hoffmann and his cabinet did not dare remain in Munich. They took refuge in Bamberg, a conservative Catholic stronghold, and from there they appealed urgently for help from the Reich government and from other German states.

A large number of Bavarian farmers and rural landowners opposed the Council Republic. So too did the urban wealthy and devout Catholic circles. The Council regime did not, however, take over the industries, the banks, or other economic key points. During the night of April 12/13 a new shift brought Communists into an Action Committee, which replaced the former Central Council. It picked a four-man executive group headed by a Communist, Eugene Leviné. By this time the region controlled by the Council Republic was being blockaded by the supporters of the Hoffmann government and of the Ebert regime in Berlin. The action group issued orders aimed at disarming the Bavarian bourgeoisie, placing workers in key positions in industry, and nationalizing the banks. Commissions were established to control the economy, transportation, and communications (especially the press, which was a thorn in the flesh of the Council Republic supporters).

Leaders of the Independent Socialists soon succeeded in reversing some of the measures supported by Communists in the Action Committee. Thereupon, the Communists resigned from the Committee. Its head, the Independent Socialist Ernst Toller, a gifted young dramatist and poet, sought unsuccessfully to negotiate with the Hoffmann cabinet in Bamberg.

By April 30, Noske had ringed Munich with military and paramilitary forces estimated at some 60,000 armed troops. On May 1, as Marut's historic report reveals, they penetrated important sectors of the city. Some resistance continued as long as May 3, but on May 4 the last of the defenders of the Bavarian Council Republic were crushed in the outskirts of Munich.

Martial law was declared from the start of the action. Hundreds of defending soldiers, students, workers, and intellectuals were killed outright or beaten. More than 2,000 arrested persons were sentenced to terms in penitentiaries and prisons. Among the officers directing the crushing of the Bavarian Council Republic were a number who, a few years later, became prominent aides of Adolf Hitler in the German Nazi movement. One such was General Franz Epp, soon to be the Nazi specialist for "colonial problems." After Hitler became Chancellor late in January, 1933, Epp was elevated to the post of the *Führer*'s deputy, or *Statthalter,* for Bavaria. Another was Captain Ernst Röhm, later the head of the Nazi storm troopers, a hard-bitten homosexual, slaughtered finally on Hitler's order in the bloody purge of June, 1934.

By no means all those killed or wounded in early May, 1919, were members or even supporters of the Council Republic, or of the Eisner regime that had preceded it. More than twenty people were killed, for example, in the meeting place of a Catholic organization by invaders who mistakenly took them to be Spartacists. The reactionary wave that engulfed Bavaria following these events made it, more than any other German state, the most favorable breeding ground for the Nazi movement.

Marut's highly individual report, here appearing in English for the first time, focuses the light of an incandescent indignation on many of these events.

In the Freest State in the World [*]

It is not only the freest state in the world but it also has the freest voting system in the world. A voting system that enables the man who owns one—or twenty—large newspapers, or who takes the trouble to have several million cleverly gotten-up leaflets printed and distributed, to gain as much influence on the election as he desires. A voting system which permits the church confessional and the pulpit, the marital bed and the death bed, to be used for purposes of political propaganda, is indeed the freest voting system on earth.

It has been demonstrated that those who vote for the Social Democratic Party are composed approximately one-third of women and two-thirds of men. The voters for the official Christ-desecrators,[1] on the other hand, are two-thirds women and one-third men. And such a voting system passes for the will of the people.

The freest state in the world indeed: profiteers, usurers, and racketeers, killer-robbers and murderers of revolutionaries, all are living a life of luxury and debauchery. Workers

[*] Translated from the German of Ret Marut
by Mina C. and H. Arthur Klein

and revolutionaries, on the other hand, are being slaughtered
and martyred in jails and penitentiaries.

That all this would happen if ever the Social Democrats
came to power, I told Social Democratic workers as long ago
as the year 1905.[2] That the Social Democrats, once in power,
would be a hundred times more brutal than the fathers of the
Anti-Socialist Laws,[3] I told Social Democratic workers in
1907. I told them this not out of political understanding
(which I did not have then and do not have today, that being
the reason I have been able to retain my feeling for human
beings); rather I told it to them out of the feeling that Social
Democracy was breeding a popery worse than that of the
Catholic Church.

And so today it has, in fact, come to pass: Social Democracy, which asserts that it is based on the materialist conception of history, is totally blind with regard to the inevitable
and logical course of historical developments. Social Democracy believed that it alone was *the* revolutionary party; it believed that it alone represented the interests of the workers; it
believed that it was the be-all and end-all of all political development. And yet, apparent to all who were willing to see,
there came into being even many years before World War I,
the successor to Social Democracy: the Communist Party.[4]

So, now, as a result, the Social Democratic Party has become the conservative party in this country, because with astonishment and fright it realizes that it is constantly being
driven from positions on the left, ever further toward positions on the right. And we must surely keep our eyes wide
open, because the Communist Party has at *its* left its extremely strong successor; and it may be that the Communist
Party, once in power, will perhaps persecute the supporters of
its successor party just as today the Communists are perse-
cuted by the Social Democrats.

I stand—to continue using a political concept—so far to
the left that my breath does not even stir that successor to the
Communist Party.[5]

The only person who could smile at this is one who forgets that humanity unceasingly evolves onward, and that human history, like nature, shows no static moments.

But to what a state of degeneracy this Social Democratic Party has sunk, which hunts down like wild animals in the forest revolutionaries and workers who ask nothing but the fulfillment of what was promised to them a thousand times by the rulers of today—promised in the days before they began to rule. Indeed, it is worse, for the animals of the forest are granted periods of closed seasons, and skilled hunting is required at other times.

How depraved this Party has become which offers bounties of 10,000 and 30,000 marks for the capture of fleeing revolutionaries, the purpose being not to protect the population from them, but rather to wreak vengeance on them and murder them. What more can you expect from this Party whose members perpetrate murders on revolutionaries—legal murders, which they call death sentences. And this in a country where, since 1848, and despite the Anti-Socialist Laws, no death sentence has been carried out against revolutionaries.

How must honest workers regard this Party whose leaders in Bavaria alone throw five thousand revolutionaries into prison, and hand down pentitentiary sentences as long as fifteen years and eight years—this Party whose founders and leaders themselves once received asylum in Switzerland and England, but whose present leaders, in the most brutal and vicious manner, demand the extradition of fugitive revolutionaries who have sought and found protection in foreign countries. The purpose of these demands is vengeance —base vengeance.

The Party which, despite the monstrous misery of the German people, can produce untold tens of millions of marks in order to wreak cruel vengeance on revolutionaries, has thereby proclaimed its decay and disintegration.

In addition to the many old lies of the Party bosses,[6] thousands of new lies are added: "We are not the government; the government is a coalition."

Good. But if the Party bigwigs, in consequence of this brutal vengeance (which with their silent approval is being

wreaked against revolutionaries) were to quit the coalition—
which, in any case, is a mockery of socialist ideas—then the
unprecedented crimes against the revolutionaries would no
longer be possible. And Social Democrats, whose program
calls for abolition of the death penalty, are voting for death
penalties to be carried out. But they lie again, saying that they
did not vote *for* this. Had they voted against it, the murders of
revolutionaries could not be carried out. And now again, as
during the war, they abstained from voting, and in this way
did not openly violate their Party's platform. Up to now, actions of this kind were attributed only to the Jesuits.

Such a Party is being guided in a way that abandons
revolutionaries to the lust for vengeance and the bloodthirstiness of a degenerate and bestial bourgeoisie. Thus, the
Party has done more damage to the concept of the nation than
ever could have been done by a revolutionary. And only as a
result of this was it possible that in Munich seven revolutionaries (not to mention more respectable men and women) received neither pardon nor amnesty, but rather were legally
murdered a few hours after their trials—whereas in the same
city, four days later, a hold-up man who had slain a tavern-
keeper and his wife while committing a theft, was pardoned;
and people who had tortured their own children in the most
brutal and gruesome way were sentenced to only a few days
in jail.

And you think that the German Revolution is not coming?

Spartacists[7] are not the ones who are making the
Revolution in Germany, but rather those here who utter the
lie that they must protect the German people from the Revolution—it is *they* who are making the Revolution.

But woe to you, officers, soldiers, Party bosses, judges,
state's attorneys, informers, and newspaper-scribblers,[8] who
have murdered and martyred revolutionaries! You have
handed down your own sentences. Your deaths are decided,
and I believe that even I am no longer able to rescue you. If I
can, however—if I have even a trace of opportunity to save
you—I shall do it, because to me human blood is precious
above all else.

How many people were there who hoped that the bourgeoisie would be better, nobler, more just and more conciliatory than the Spartacists? I, too, cherished this hope—I, even more than others, because I believe there is goodness in a person as long as he still retains a breath of life. But how disappointed we were! The unleashed bourgeoisie, whom we believed had attained a loftier level of culture, was, in fact, more bestial, more avid for vengeance, and more bloodthirsty than Spartacus ever had been even for an instant.

How much you would have won, citizens, had you but shown only a trace of magnanimity and conciliation! You would have, perhaps, gained a lifelong reprieve. But as it is, you have yourselves determined your own decline and fall, perhaps your total annihilation. And that is a pity; because among you are many who are capable of salvaging great and undying values.

But among the newspaper-scribblers, there is no one who could preserve or create intellectual values or cultural treasures among the people of the future.

Since order has been restored on the corpses of about six hundred honest revolutionaries[9]—(I greet you all again in death! All of you, without a single exception, not even excepting the so-called "murderers of hostages." All of you died for the sacred cause of human progress; and all of us make mistakes)—insecurity in the city of Munich has reached its peak. And this has happened in spite of the fact that international Social Democracy expelled more than twenty thousand aliens (among whom they included also Prussians, Saxons, and Württembergers), and placed "unreliable elements" under protective arrest or simply tossed them into jail. Nevertheless, since the restoration of order in Munich, more robbery-murders and sex-murders have been committed than in the five years preceding the temporary end of the Bavarian Council[10] Republic.

Among these killings, six remain unsolved out of those committed during the few months of the bayonet-based "order." This is quite natural, for robbery-murderers and rapists are having happy days in Munich, ever since the entire force of law-enforcement officials, policemen, police inform-ers, and minions of the law of the Hoffmann-Noske-Epp[11] dictatorship is busy searching for escaped revolutionaries; and a whole horde of them are roaming around in Switzerland, in Austria, and in Prussia, so that to the many tens of millions of marks of past police expenses, several additional tens of millions must be added.

In the bright light of noonday in the busiest streets of Munich, stores are robbed bare, because the police and their informers have eyes only for Spartacus people. This time, the murderers and the plunderers can't be Spartacus people, be-cause the latter are lying dead, buried in cemeteries or in some sandpit they were hurriedly thrown into. Those that re-main alive are serving time in jails and prisons. Nor can they be aliens from outside Bavaria, because these without excep-tion have been expelled.

Nor, this time, can it be Jews who once again "are upset-ting order," because the Jews—as their leaders have pro-claimed to the Aryans in shameful public statements—have "stoutly cooperated in the liberation of the dear city of Mu-nich from the red terror of Russian Bolshevists, and have con-tributed their property and their blood in order to help the le-gitimate Hoffmann government regain its ascendancy."

While Bavaria is now the freest state in the freest coun-try in the world, Prussia merely lays claim to being the freest state in the world with the freest voting system in the world. For this reason it was possible that, in Prussia, in the city of Lyck in East Prussia (which is subject to the authority of the Social Democrat August Winnig),[12] a friend of the *Ziegel-brenner*[13] periodical was sentenced to two years' fortress-imprisonment[14] because, with the permission of the *Ziegel-brenner*'s editor, he had duplicated and distributed as a re-print several hundred copies of the first article in volume 16/17. An article which carries the title "The New World War"—an article whose sole content is justice and humanity.

I learned of this shameful action only a few days ago; for the time being I feel it is my duty to work for the downfall of the government that perpetrated so shameful an act. But I greet that revolutionary comrade: his imprisonment will not last a day longer than that of the "dishonorable" Dr. Wadler,[15] who by rights ought to serve eight years in the penitentiary; and than that of the "honorable" Erich Mühsam,[16] who could spend fifteen years in fortress confinement—if it came to that, and if Scheidemann[17] were not a liar, and if Noske were not a German.[18]

Among all of those who became known to me through M[19] (and the "dishonorable" Dr. Leviné,[20] T. Axelrod,[21] and Dr. Wadler are among them), there is also only one who could really be called dishonorable if I were to apply the standards of bourgeois morality. But about this matter I shall speak later on, so fully that all the peoples of the earth will hear.

I am a little hampered in my work. Several hundred letters are on hand awaiting answers to the question, "How goes it with Ret Marut?" From friends of the *Ziegelbrenner* I have received so many splendid letters asking about my colleague M, and about aid and support for M— some of our supporters, unsolicited, sent sums of money for M— that I lack any words with which to express thanks. I would hurt those people, if I were to tell what I felt on reading most of their letters.

I am hampered in all my activities: The *Ziegelbrenner* publishing house has been as good as destroyed by the officers of the dictatorship-democracy of Noske-Hoffmann-Epp-Möhl. Its remnants are scattered in five different rooms, far removed from each other. Orders cannot be filled. My most trusted collaborator,[22] without whose tireless activity I am almost helpless is being hunted on a warrant for high treason issued by the Bavarian government, and is in flight from the bloodthirsty royal Wittelsbach Social Democrats,[23] somewhere in a decent foreign country[24] which does not claim for itself the title of the freest state in the world.

As a result of all this, the *Ziegelbrenner* is written by an editorial staff on the run and published by a press in flight. More than four hundred impatient subscribers have in the meantime canceled their subscriptions. I am not depressed because of this; the ranks of the *Ziegelbrenner* supporters in

consequence will only become that much more pure as the superfluous ones withdraw and go back to where they came
from—to the prostitute press.

It was May 1, 1919,[25] labor's first worldwide May Day
since the November 1918 farce,[26] which the Social Democrats
claim was a revolution, and about which they lie and bam-
boozle all the peoples of the earth. On that afternoon of May
1, a meeting of revolutionary and freedom-loving writers
from all over Germany was to be held.

My co-worker M was also invited to this writers' meeting, partly because of his position as the editorial head of
Der Ziegelbrenner, but principally because of his role as a
member of the Propaganda Commission of the Council Republic of Bavaria.

According to the contents of the warrants for his arrest,
the high treason that M committed and which led to the issu-
ance of those warrants, consisted in the fact that M belonged
to the Preparatory Commission for the formation of the Revolutionary Tribunal, and to the Propaganda Commission. For
this reason he was made the object of arrest warrants issued by
the Bavarian government which sought to throw him into jail
for about fifteen years, or—if dishonorable intentions could
be proved against him (which the shameful judges of Bavaria
can manage by a mere twist of the wrist, as the trials have pub-
licly shown even to the most obstinate reactionaries)—to murder him legally.

I declare here and now: Until this hour there has never
been anywhere on earth a court in which all judgments were
handed down with such deep human understanding of every
human act, as in this Revolutionary Tribunal of the Council
Republic, which is described as a horror-court by the Bavarian government and its press pimps. The fact that this so-called
"horror-court" was guided by so lofty a concept of the role of
a court is due, not least, to the accomplishments of M, who—
and this I am imparting to the state's attorneys of Bavaria, because until now they have not known it—was unanimously
elected by the Preparatory Commission of the court as its
presiding officer and speaker.

The Provisional Revolutionary Central Council of the Council Republic of Bavaria had unanimously assigned M to this Commission. In the Convention of Factory Councils, which exercised the highest governmental authority of the Council Republic of Bavaria, M was unanimously elected to the Propaganda Commission—in fact, he was nominated by a printer who works for a bourgeois newspaper.

M still declares today, and he always will, that this election by revolutionary factory councils represented for him the highest honor, and for his labors the highest recognition, which has come to him between the time of the masquerade of November 1918 and the present.

In all his tasks—for he held no offices—which were entrusted to him by the revolutionary workers, he stood for those same ideas that can be found expressed in the *Ziegelbrenner*. The fact that, because of these tasks—which he, as a revolutionary, felt bound to take on, and which it would have been indecent and counterrevolutionary to refuse—M is now pursued for high treason like a wild animal, and is robbed of food and shelter, gives a clearer picture of the freest state in the world than do all the articles in the newspapers.

As M was sitting in the Maria Theresia Coffee House on the Augusten Strasse, where he hoped to meet several participants in a writers' meeting, the autos carrying the white-guardists[27] began to dash through the streets, bent on "liberating" Munich from the red terror. The white-guardists did not begin by making statements; they fired mercilessly with machine guns directly into crowds of people who were walking the streets dressed in their Sunday best.

At once, seven innocent citizens lay wallowing in their blood on Augusten Strasse. Two of them died then and there. A seriously wounded well-dressed man lay on the street a few steps from the coffee house. While the machine-gun fire of the white-guardists continued to rage, M, together with a few helpful people, carried the unconscious wounded man into the coffee house.

A woman doctor who was in the coffee house managed to locate the wound only after a lengthy examination. It turned out to be an uncommonly severe injury to the main artery of the left thigh. After an emergency bandage had been applied, an ambulance arrived which picked up the wounded and dead from the street and also took the injured man from the coffee house.

Then the coffee house was closed, and M left the building. He had walked scarcely a few hundred steps—the streets were still under fire from the white-guardists—when an auto dashed madly up. It was loaded with about sixty infantry weapons and rifles on which about ten clerks and students were sitting, all wearing white armbands and handkerchiefs wrapped around their sleeves.

When they saw and recognized M, they stopped their car. Five of them rushed from the car at M. They had rifles slung around their shoulders and a revolver in each hand, plus four to six hand grenades at their belts. They pointed their revolvers at M and bellowed at him, "Hands up!"

M asked what these gentlemen wanted of him. They said to him that he was a member of the Central Committee, the most dangerous agitator in the Council Republic, the scourge of the citizenry, and the destroyer of the press. Hence, they said, they had to take him along, and if he did not admit that he bore the primary guilt for the bloodbath now being carried out, then they'd have to make quick work of him.

M was then searched for weapons by each and every one of these bloodthirsty ruffians. The editorial head of *Der Ziegelbrenner* was searched for weapons! Naturally, you can also search for truffles on bare paving stones, if you have nothing else to do.

On M was found an ordinary housekey, which, however, to the astonishment of these half-baked clowns, was not usable as a weapon!

When M now asked where these noble liberators and defenders-of-law-and-order carried the legal warrant for his arrest, the rest of the fellows, who still sat in the auto, pointed their pistols at him.

M then asked these brave liberators to allow him to go to his house once more, in order to take care of his most urgent affairs before his arrest and possible death. Thereupon he was searched once again for weapons and machine guns, and then thrown violently into the auto on top of the rifles.

In the meantime, a number of pedestrians had gathered around to watch the incident. The white-guardists became aware of them and began to denounce M loudly, saying that he was the one principally responsible for the human blood that had been shed and was still to be shed; but that he was now about to get what was coming to him.

These incitements had no effect at all on the crowd. Only one of those present said quite loudly, "That is M." And the bystanders asked, in turn, "So? That is M?"

As a result of this public declaration of neutrality, it was not possible for the white-guardists to stand M against a wall then and there and shoot him down. Hence, the noble "freedom-fighters" and saviors of the bourgeoisie dashed away in their auto, shouting, carrying with them M, surrounded by ten pistols and rifles pointed straight at him.

Wherever they spied people on the streets, these brave boys yelled, "Now we've really nabbed one of them—the most dangerous one of all!"

Even though these bold liberators *were* liberators, and, as such, surely had a feeble notion of human pride and freedom, they nevertheless felt they had to get official approval before they could proceed. For, as they passed one of the more imposing houses, they spied a man standing in an upper window. In spite of the menace of M and the danger that he might perhaps escape from them, they stopped their car, stood up as erect as they could, drew themselves to attention, removed their hats, and resoundingly bellowed, "Long live *der Herr General:* Hurrah, hurrah, hurrah!!!"

Their joy and gratification at being once again underlings for a moment, and able to roar out praise to an oppressor of humanity, seemed to make them forget completely their usual subservience, for after their hurrahs at stiff attention were over, they called up to him:

"Herr General, now we've got one of them here—the most dangerous one of all!"

The Herr General—whose presence and placid appearance in his house served as sufficient indication of the extent of Bolshevist terror—waved a benevolent greeting from on high. Deeply gratified, as if each one had been promoted to the rank of Prussian top sergeant, the honest battlers for Munich's liberation dashed off, bearing with them their valuable prey.

They stopped in front of the War Ministry[28] building. Under heavy guard, M was dragged from the car, searched again for weapons, and then was led through a hundred-yard-long corridor lined by heavily armed war profiteers, bourgeois sonny-boys, elegant pimps, and such hangers-on of the hodgepodge collection that calls itself the middle class and respectable officialdom. All of them wanted to play at revolution, now that it was safe to do so—now that the infamous army troops had set up their field camp in front of the *Residenz*[29] and had begun to occupy public buildings.

M was placed in confinement in one of the rear rooms of the War Ministry building. A kind of attorney's clerk, or something similar, had the job of guarding this room. He was asked by the heroes who delivered M there, "Do you have weapons too?"

"Here, see for yourself!"—and with that the guard pulled a Browning out of each of his pants pockets, showed them to the prisoner, showed him further that each was loaded, and held them close under his nose while releasing their safety catches.

"I'd just like to see him try to escape," said this guard, while M's captors looked at M as if he were a well-fattened calf whose slaughter they awaited with almost unbearable impatience.

Now began the judicial examination or questioning of M. For a while, the gentlemen bickered back and forth as to which one of them was best qualified to conduct such a hearing. And when the examination then began, first one, then another, would break in with shouts of "Aw, you don't know how to question! Let me do it a while!"

So it went for a good long time, until finally all of them at once were questioning M.

The examination consisted of accusing M of about

twenty serious crimes of high treason: incitement of soldiers
against their officers, insulting the leaders of the Social Democratic Party, use of force and violence against the legitimate
Hoffmann government of Bavaria, and various other infamous acts, for which—according to the wishes of the
Social Democrat Hoffmann—the death penalty was to be
carried out forthwith.

M explained that he had nothing to say here, and that,
in particular, he could not recognize as judges or magistrates
these gentlemen who with violence had simply dragged him, a
peaceful pedestrian, off the street.

As nothing could be forced out of M, one of the gentlemen suddenly screamed, "Make a voluntary confession! We're
now going to fetch the witnesses, and then—so much the worse
for you!—then we'll really finish you off, once and for all!"

And soon witnesses arrived who testified to everything desired of them. These witnesses, who were always at hand, especially when they were permitted to witness a worker being
stood against a fence and shot, also played important roles in
the trials conducted by the infamous Bavarian courts,[30] whose
operations will provide better and more valuable evidence in
days to come of the bestiality, the brutality, the hypocrisy,
and the degeneracy of the German bourgeoisie than do the
War and the Lie of November 1918.[31]

Witnesses for his defense were named by M, who sought
to have them called; but his requests were disregarded here,
just as similar requests were later disregarded by those infamous Bavarian courts.

After his captors had got nowhere, they went in search
of further adventures. M was left under the strict surveillance
of the Browning-pistol-wielder. After half an hour, the same
company of heroes trooped in again. In spite of their repeated
threats, M continued to have nothing to say to them, and they
declared they would now force him to confess.

M, now flanked by two heavily armed guards, and followed by two more, was led back again through the corridor
of armed men outside the War Ministry building, and taken
to the *Residenz*.

The situation in the streets had now changed completely. From the windows waved blue-white flags;[32] on public buildings, where formerly had fluttered socialist banners—long since betrayed and besmirched by Social Democracy—black-white-red[33] flags of Imperial Germany were now displayed.

Although Herr Hoffmann's jailers (whose feeding trough was now beginning to grow full) called out to the lanes of bystanders around the War Ministry and also around the *Residenz* that they were bringing in an arrested Spartacist, M was neither struck nor reviled by any of the vigilantes. But in other parts of the city at this time, things were proceeding in a more bestial manner.[34]

Once in the *Residenz,* M was turned over to soldiers of the infamous army,[35] while his captors and the witnesses against him sought permission to remain with M, to prevent him from escaping, and so that they would be right on hand when M was placed before the court-martial.

After half an hour, the order was given that M was to be taken to Police Headquarters where one court-martial was at work. But downstairs, as M was about to be taken away, he and his escort were not allowed out of the door of the *Residenz* because, in the meantime, a counterorder had come: to place him directly before the court-martial at work in the *Residenz* itself.

M was led back again into the anteroom of a large hall in which the court-martial was in session. The court-martial in this freest state of the world consisted of one dashing lieutenant. He disposed of every case in about three minutes. On the basis of denunciations by informers he decided whether the arrestee was to be summarily shot at once, or set free. In cases of doubt, the arrestee was shot—because that was safer. No time was allowed to let defense witnesses be brought, or even to summon people who could confirm that the arrestee was no Spartacist, let alone a leader of Spartacists.

The hall in which M now found himself became increasingly full of captured workers, red-guards, sailors, girls, and boys. Among the other denounced people there, M saw a sixteen-year-old boy who was charged with having attacked soldiers of the infamous army and with having spread Spartacist propaganda.

At every moment, workers and sailors with deadly white faces were led out of the large hall in which the cigarette-smoking lieutenant decided on life or death for the prisoners. Their horror-struck and tragic eyes revealed to the others who waited that they had received death sentences.

Probably when this is written it will no longer be possible to determine whether the lieutenant who decided the fate of the Spartacists and the denounced members of the Council Republic was assigned to the office by the Hoffmann government, or whether he had simply installed himself in it on his own.

So passed an hour of excruciating waiting. M asked his guards whether he might still write a note to his friends to inform them where he was. This was refused him. At that point, the man who was to be tried by the lieutenant just before M, was summoned and led in. This man was seized so violently by the mercenaries that he resisted loudly and vigorously. In the confusion that resulted, M succeeded in escaping. Not unconnected with M's escape were two soldiers, in whom for an instant a spark of humanity arose as they saw what was being done here to the most precious of human possessions—human life. Let them be thanked at this point for preserving a man's life.

In the army of infamy, according to my estimates, there are about ten thousand misled soldiers and officers of the Reichswehr. Soldiers and officers of the Reichswehr are recognizable by the fact that they are human beings and not subject to Noske's orders. But the Reichswehr, too, is unnecessary and superfluous for the German people; and Germany will have the right to say that Goethe is a German only when in all Germany no firearms, no hand grenades, and no gas bombs can be found, excepting in a museum.

It was, in fact, a Reichswehr officer who, in a public bar in Munich, said to a gentleman who until then was not acquainted with *Der Ziegelbrenner,* "To me Munich is the best-loved city among all cities that I know, because the *Ziegel-brenner* is published in it."

(During the war, the *Ziegelbrenner* had among its sub-scribers about three hundred army officers, many of whom were in active correspondence with its editor.)

Since that hour in which M managed to escape, he has been in flight. We have many times considered whether it would not be better for M to place himself voluntarily in the power of the courts, for in the long run it is no particular plea-sure to spend many nights in forests, barns and haylofts, and empty houses, in order not to be interned, and finally be turned over after all to the authorities.

However, it would simply mean increasing this public German infamy if an honest revolutionary were to place him-self voluntarily in the hands of these courts, which now—as if to fill the measure of outrage to overflowing—call themselves "people's courts." For it has been revealed ever more clearly and crassly—especially since the reactionary forces think they again have power in their hands for a long time (the workers having become smarter in not believing a suitable time for them is as yet at hand)—that the courts of Germany are no genuine courts, but rather are institutions of cruelest vengeance and bloodthirstiness; that the judges are no judges, but rath-er are venal executioners and puppets of capitalism and the bourgeoisie; that the judges are not just and judicious men, but members of monarchist parties and members of the Catholic Center Party[36] and of the "democratic" cliques; that the judi-cial procedures are only spectacles for the prostitute press, so that even some ordinary journalists have become disgusted; and that these judicial procedures are only supposed to pro-vide clever state's attorneys with opportunities to set off bril-liant fireworks, and be praised for it by the prostitute press be-cause, according to that press, in their accusations the state's attorneys allow no place for feelings of humanity, but rather bring down just punishment upon common criminals.

The Revolution is following its unalterable course; it is

proceeding onward inevitably and irresistibly; and such a reactionary power, so bestial an army of infamy, such unjust
and inhuman judges must first appear, in order to prepare the
soil for the future German Revolution. The state of blindness
that today afflicts the bourgeoisie and the bloodthirstiness and
vengeance-seeking with which it attempts to stabilize its shaky
position, is a necessary prerequisite for that which is to come.

The bourgeoisie has not abolished capital punishment;
rather it has extended it even further to include political offenders. I wish honestly from my heart and out of pure humanity that the rejection of the proposal to abolish capital
punishment does not boomerang and have more far-reaching
results for the bourgeoisie than hitherto for the proletariat.
The German bourgeoisie has forfeited every moral right to be
cast aside without the use of violence and murder. If the proletariat nevertheless does manage without bloodshed to ad-
minister the *coup de grâce* to the degenerate bourgeoisie—
and the proletariat has the strength to do this, because it pos-
sesses greater morality and humanity in its soul—then the victory of the coming Revolution will be made that much more
certain and permanent.

It will soon be reported (here in *Der Ziegelbrenner*)
what happened to the *Ziegelbrenner* publishing office and to
its friends, after the events perpetrated in the name of the
freest state in the world and in the name of its "democratic"
dictators. This delay in reporting is necessary because the records are not yet complete, and every day brings down upon us
additional "freedom" and additional "order."

The Council Republic is not the culmination of everything, and even less does it stand for the most perfect form in
which humans can live together. However, the Council Republic is a prerequisite for the reconstruction of culture, because it makes possible the liquidation of the state. It must be
the task of the revolutionary of today to work for the Council
system and with it also for the Council Republic.

Consequently you will understand that M, immediately
after his escape, and as long as he still had the slightest free-

dom of action, took with him into the Bavarian countryside the principles of the Council Republic and the idea of the Council system.

In about sixty cities, villages, and localities of Bavaria, he talked with citizens, peasants, and workers. He elected to use a different method from that which has become usual today —a method that is more successful: he used a form of persuasion which is the only one that produces worthwhile results, a form that is very old and that was also used by Christ— namely, talking person to person, talking to the smallest gatherings or groups of people. His listeners rarely numbered more than twelve persons at a time.

But from these intimate conversations, which were in every way informal and unstructured, and which gave every listener opportunities through counterquestioning to become completely clear about what M had said, no citizen, no worker, no peasant went away who had not recognized the big lie called "democracy" for what it is—namely, a big lie.

It was by no means M's intention that every listener should leave a convinced, enthusiastic Council republican. Such speedy enthusiasms and speedily acquired convictions are seldom the salt to be used as seasoning in cases like these.

Often M traveled for three days in succession to the same place in order to fulfill his task there. Never has he been denounced to the authorities, either by a citizen or by a peasant, although his listeners can hardly have been in doubt as to his identity.

By means solely of large political meetings, probably no one has been so completely won over to so novel a thing as the Council system that he could say he learned exactly what the Council system is, what it aims at, and how it operates. That is the reason such terrible confusion exists among workers—because, as a result of insufficient knowledge, every worker has a different conception of the meaning of the Council system, the Council Republic, and the dictatorship of the proletariat.

The real need is not to persuade the great masses, to whip them up to flaming enthusiasm, to move them to adopt a resolution. Rather the great need is to convince individual human beings. The people of the future, and the people who are preparing for that which is to come, should not be argued into this without thinking things out; they should not believe unconditionally; rather they should be filled with the consciousness that this Revolution is right and feasible, whereas that other bourgeois order is wrong and not feasible. The people who today carry within them the will to future development, should not work for the coming society by relying on the mind of a clever *Führer,* but rather with their own minds, with their own hearts, and with their own souls.

But this they can do only when they know what it is all about, and when they also know and understand exactly what they themselves want.

When workers and peasants—and not greedy bourgeois —first truly come to understand the Council system and its values and its way of working, then any other form of human living-together and working-together during the period of transition to a higher form of society will seem nonsensical to them.

Among his listeners M met a citizen active in the academic world, who said he was a decided opponent of the Council system, and who, with a weapon in his hand, had taken part enthusiastically in overthrowing the Council Republic. After the conclusion of a conversation with M, this gentleman said that M had not persuaded him, but that he wanted to reflect further on what he had heard. Two months later, M again met the man. The first thing he said to M was, "You are right, and for several weeks now I have been a fully convinced supporter of the Council Republic."

M mentions this case because it is, to date, the only instance in which M had the opportunity to speak again with an opponent, not immediately after a conversation, but several weeks later.

Notes to Ret Marut's
In the Freest State in the World

by Mina C. and H. Arthur Klein

1. "the official Christ-desecrators," in Marut's arsenal of epithets, refers to the leaders of the Catholic Party of Bavaria, once known as the Center (German: *Zentrum*), later calling itself the Bavarian People's Party (BVP).

2. "year 1905" may seem an improbably early date for the man who became Ret Marut and then B. Traven to have been active and politically informed in Germany. Yet it is possible. Shreds of evidence, which cannot be detailed here, suggest that by 1905 he was in his early twenties, and actively involved in workingclass politics.

3. The Anti-Socialist laws were pushed through the *Reichstag* by Bismarck in 1878, after the Socialist Party (SPD) had won 500,000 votes and elected twelve delegates to that body. The laws, draconically framed and rigorously applied, broke up the Socialists' organizations, trade unions, newspapers, and publishing centers. Nevertheless the movement resisted and ultimately staged a comeback, gaining 35 *Reichstag* delegates by 1890, and 89 by 1903. In the Germany of 1919, of course, the Anti-Socialist laws were only a memory, but of a nightmare kind, to the readers Marut hoped he would reach with this piece.

4. "Communist Party" here cannot mean the Communist Party of Germany (KPD), which did not come into being under that name until the start of 1919, when it arose out of the militant Spartacist Bund. Marut here means rather the Majority Socialists of Russia, known since 1903 as the Bolsheviki or Bolshevists. They, however, adopted the Communist Party name during 1918, only a year prior to the one in which Marut wrote this piece for the *Ziegelbrenner*.

5. "successor to the Communist Party"—seems typically cryptic and obscure. Very likely Marut meant that all things change, particularly in political struggles. He had flaunted his independence of *all* parties in a fiery proclamation issued nearly a year earlier, declaring: "I do not belong to the Social Democratic Party, nor am I an Independent Socialist. I do not belong to the Spartacus group, nor am I a Bolshevik. I belong to no party, to no political association of any description. . . . I cannot belong to any party, because I see in any party membership a limitation of my personal freedom; because the pledge to a party program takes from me . . . that which I regard as the highest and noblest goal on earth: to be allowed to be a human being."

6. "Party bosses" here and "Party bigwigs" below translate Marut's term *Partei-Pfaffen,* literally "Party priests"—meaning the officials of the German Social Democratic Party who —in his view—misled and swindled their followers as priests mislead and swindle the faithful.

7. "Spartacists" entered German political history when, after January, 1916, a small but gifted group of militant Socialists began publishing a series called Spartacus Letters, designed to free the enslaved minds of German workers as the original Spartacus had sought to free Roman slaves in 72 B.C.E. The

Spartacist leaders and agitators after the spring of 1917 were reinforced by the Independent Socialists, but the former retained their organizational autonomy, and by the end of 1918 metamorphosed into the new German Communist Party. During 1919, "Spartacist" became a scareword to the German bourgeoisie and even to the orthodox Majority Socialists (SPD), who largely controlled the new government. It was the domestic equivalent of Bolshevik during the same era in western Europe and the U.S.A.

8. "newspaper-scribblers" is a justified translation of Marut's phrase, *Zeitungs-schreiber,* for here and in many other key writings he vented burning contempt on "the press" and those who served it.

9. "six hundred" is not far beyond the official figures of deaths resulting from the violent crushing of the Bavarian Council Republic at the beginning of May, 1919. Known deaths totaled 599 in and around Munich, of which less than ten percent were those of the invading troops and vigilante groups. Of the remainder—deaths among the defeated defenders—great numbers did not fall while fighting but were killed after capture: either beaten to death or shot without trial, or after the most summary drumhead court-martial, later acknowledged to have been illegal.

"Hostages," in the following sentence, refers to an event that turned many against the defenders of the Council Republic in Bavaria. Its so-called Red Army, during April, arrested and imprisoned a number of leading royalists and reactionaries, including some of the "Thule Society," implicated in the incitement that resulted in the assassination of Kurt Eisner. As the invading anti-Red troops ringed Munich, Commandant Rudolf Egelhofer, military head of the defending Red guards, ordered these prisoners killed. Some twenty were slain before Ernst Toller, the then political head, managed to stop the slaughter. These killings were widely reported as an atrocity. R. M. Watt, an authority on the period, has concluded that "The Munich revolutionaries had talked about terror a great deal more than they had practised it. Not so the *Freikorps.*" And he notes also that "The white terror which followed was vastly more savage than anything the Communists had undertaken."

10. "Council Republic"—the German phrase is *Räte-Republik.* Many of the histories translate this as "Soviet Republic" or even simply "Soviet" of Bavaria. This is not downright wrong but is misleading. *Rat* (singular) and *Räte* (plural) are ancient words, deeply rooted in Germany's past, and antedating (in this sense) the example of the Russian Soviets from 1917 onward, or even from 1905. *Rat* has the double sense of an assembly or council, and of counsel or advice.

11. See Introduction, p. 155.

12. August Winnig was a Social Democratic officeholder of no special importance. To Marut, he was just one more example of the despised Party bosses or "party-priests."

13. See Introduction, p. 155.

14. "fortress-imprisonment" is the German *Festungshaft,* or detention in a fortress—a distinctly less dishonorable and uncomfortable kind of incarceration that *Zuchthaus,* which corresponds roughly to penitentiary, or even than *Gefängnis,* which is like ordinary jail. Sentences passed on persons convicted for acts they had done during the days of the Bavarian Council Republic (November, 1918 through April, 1919), included 905 condemnations to such fortress-imprisonment; 65 to *Zuchthaus;* and 1,737 to *Gefängnis.* The *Festungshaft* sentences averaged about one and a half years; the *Zuchthaus* sentences, however, more than five times that long.

15. Dr. Wadler, an Independent Socialist and a former German Army officer, had been Minister of Housing in the Eisner cabinet in Bavaria after November 7, 1918. He is one of the few government officials known to have met Ret Marut face to face during the period between then and the terrible finale, in the first days of May, 1919. The ironic term "dishonorable" as used here seems to show that, so far as Marut knew when he wrote these lines, Wadler had not been granted the benefit of a fortress-confinement type of sentence, reserved for those whose acts the court considered to have been "honorable" in origin. However, the complete meaning of this paragraph remains cryptic and probably was intended to be so.

16. Erich Mühsam (1878-1934), an anarchist agitator and writer of fascinating talent and enormous courage. He took part in the original November overthrow of the royal regime in Munich, had a prominent role in the Council Republic and, after it was crushed, was sentenced to fortress confinement for five years. Early in this time—during 1922—a noteworthy postcard arrived, addressed to Mühsam. It was a greeting from his former fellowfighter Ret Marut, at that time still somewhere in Germany, and evading arrest in most extraordinary ways. Not long after his release, Mühsam published in a 1926 issue of his magazine *Fanal,* a poignant appeal, begging the vanished Ret Marut, wherever he might be, to get in touch:

> Ret Marut, comrade, friend, fellow-fighter, man—speak up, report, stir yourself, give a sign that you still live, that you are still the *Ziegelbrenner.* . . ."

Above all, Mühsam wanted to be assured that Marut had not abandoned his old convictions and loyalties. We cannot say whether the mysterious B. Traven of Mexico ever communicated in any way with Mühsam. Probably he did not. Yet Mühsam came to suspect from stylistic analyses of the B. Traven novels and stories published in Germany beginning in 1926, that this "unknown" writer, was probably identical with the *Ziegelbrenner* of those revolutionary days in Bavaria. Mühsam did not survive to learn that he had been right. He was jailed again, and subsequently murdered in horrible fashion by the Nazis, the year after Hitler became Chancellor of Germany.

17. Philipp Scheidemann (1865-1939), prominent member of the Majority Socialists (SPD) and the first Chancellor of the new Weimar Republic, between February and June, 1919. See Introduction, p. 155.

18. "If Scheidemann were not a liar, and if Noske were not a German" are puzzling phrases and probably beyond clarification at this late date. See Introduction, p. 155.

19. M— without a period! This is no typographical slip; it was deliberately printed this way by the *Ziegelbrenner*. If that letter represents Marut, or Maurhut as he sometimes chose to call himself, who, then, is the "I," of this same sentence? The "I" of the following sentence is indubitably Marut himself. Its apocalyptic and grandiose finale is assuredly in his style. Two possible answers, or guesses, can be considered. (1) The "I" here is still Marut, pretending to be someone else, because he was then wanted on a police warrant for high treason. Or, less likely, (2) it is Irene Mermet (1893-1956), Marut's longtime collaborator and companion. The manifold confusions and contradictions in *In the Freest State in the World* need not be regarded as entirely deliberate. Marut's distraught and even desperate state of mind can be sensed throughout.

20. Eugene Leviné (1883-1919), a co-founder of the German Communist Party, and a doctor of philosophy, not medicine. He was one of two similarly named but unrelated leaders of the Communist groups in Munich during April, the final month of the Council Republic. The other, also a doctor, was Max *Levien,* slightly younger than Leviné. Both had mingled Russian and German backgrounds, linguistically, educationally, and residentially. Both had been drafted into the Imperial German Army but had become Spartacists and then Communists. Leviné, after working with the brilliant Rosa Luxemburg, had come to Bavaria, reaching Munich early in March, 1919. He reorganized the local Communist Party and its executive committee; became editor of the Munich edition of the Communist newspaper, *Rote Fahne*; and devoted himself more to theory than to the rough-and-tumble of armed uprisings. He, as well as Levien, resigned from the Munich "Commune" at the end of April, as it became clear that overwhelming forces of *Freikorps* and regular troops were closing in on the city. Arrested not long after the actual penetration of Munich, Leviné was tried by a hasty court-martial, condemned to death, and shot down, his final defiant cry being "Long live the world revolution!" Levien escaped by fleeing into Austria.

21. Tobia Axelrod was another leader—or at any rate a "consultant"—of the Communists during the agitated April days of the Munich "Commune." He had been with Lenin in what was then St. Petersburg, during 1917, and had reached Germany with the staff of the first Soviet ambassador to the Imperial government in Berlin. When that ambassador was expelled from Germany, Axelrod moved to Munich where the Eisner regime was by that time installed. Late in April, as things became desperate, Axelrod was sent by airplane to seek help. His destination was either Hungary or Russia, but mechanical trouble forced down his plane still within Bavaria. After the Council Republic was smashed, Axelrod was discovered and arrested. However, his diplomatic connection saved him: from Russia came warning that if he were harmed, similar action would be taken against German diplomats there.

22. "trusted collaborator"—certainly this seems to refer to Marut himself, then "being hunted on a warrant for high treason." That suggests the "I" of these lines either was, or was meant to be understood as, Irene Mermet, who had collaborated with Marut on the *Ziegelbrenner*. (See also ftn. 19.) Conceivably the aim here was to confuse the authorities who might get hold of this issue, for M could mean Mermet as well as Marut. . . . These typical Marut/Traven riddles, layered almost endlessly like an onion, do not seem to be finally soluble, nor did Marut/Traven intend that they should be.

23. "royal Wittelsbach Social Democrats" is aimed at the leading Majority Socialists in Bavaria, such as Johannes Hoffmann, the premier who had been designated by the *Landtag* after Eisner's assassination. The phrase brands them as basically royalist and reactionary in their actions—despite their socialistic and democratic pretensions. (See Introduction, p. 155.)

24. "a decent foreign country" was probably included in order to mislead the police and their informers, who were actively searching for Ret Marut in Germany. It is virtually certain that when these words were written, printed, and posted to subscribers, Marut was still within the German boundaries, living a hunted and harassed life.

25. "It was May 1, 1919,"—here begins the narrative proper, a narrative obviously written by Marut himself but referring repeatedly to "my co-worker M," as if someone else were the writer.

26. "the November 1918 farce" refers to the events and declarations that began in Berlin on November 9 and 10, 1918 —notably, the proclamation of the German Republic, the launching of the provisional government headed by Ebert and other Majority Socialist leaders, etc. The meeting of writers mentioned in the following paragraph was, of course, to be held in Munich, not Berlin. Marut's particular role as "member of the Propaganda Commission" can be specified more precisely here. On April 7, barely more than three weeks before the seizure of Marut on May 1, he had been appointed Press Director (*Leiter*) by the revolutionary Central Council in Munich. However, in line with his repudiation of official position and formal authority, he declined, and that post went to another. Nevertheless Marut did take on the task of serving as government censor of one of the bourgeois dailies: the *Munich-Augsburg Abend-Zeitung*. The next day (April 8) the new "press representatives" (or censors) revealed a plan for the eventual socialization of the newspapers of Bavaria. Marut was the author of that plan.

27. "white-guardists" (*Weiss-Gardisten*) is what Marut called them. As during the same period in Russia, *white* here carries the sense of violently counterrevolutionary and reactionary.

28. Bavaria's "War Ministry building" stood at number 24 Ludwig Strasse, about half a mile north of the royal palace, or *Residenz,* mentioned later. During the heavy bombings of World War II, the War Ministry building was burned out.

29. The *Residenz,* at the site where Bavaria's dukes, electors, and kings had their official residences, was the showplace of old Munich. The structure to which Marut was taken was reduced to ruins by the bombings of World War II, and reconstruction began after 1945.

30. "infamous . . . courts" (*Schandgerichte*). Marut also used *Schand* as a prefix (signifying disgraceful, shameful, or outrageous) to describe the armed forces, regular or irregular, sent to crush the Bavarian Council Republic, as in *Schandwehr,* or "army of infamy."

31. "Lie of November 1918" refers again to the fraud—as Marut saw it—launched in Berlin on November 9. See ftn. 26.

32. The colors of Bavaria itself were blue and white. So too was the royal flag of the ancient house of Wittelsbach. The replacement of the red socialist banners by these flags meant reversion to royalist and reactionary principles.

33. Return to Imperial and pro-Hohenzollern sentiments was indicated by the black-white-red flags. The flag of the Weimar Republic in contrast was black-gold-red.

34. Regarding "bestial manner" see earlier notes, especially ftn. 10. Also see Introduction, p. 155.

35. For Marut's use of *Schandwehr,* here translated as "infamous army," see ftn. 30.

36. Catholic Center Party—see Introduction, p. 155.

37. Marut called them *Demokratischen Sippen* in German. This was not a denigration of principles of democracy, however. He referred here rather to the conservative, even reactionary, bourgeois groups or cliques whose chosen party names included the word "Democratic," or who claimed to espouse democratic ideals while bitterly opposing socialism, pacifism, etc.

He may well have had in mind here the German Democratic Party (DDP), and also possibly the National People's Party (NVP) and the German People's Party (DVP), as well as other and smaller conservative or right wing groups.